THE END
FIFTEEN ENDINGS TO FIFTEEN PAINTINGS

Short fiction inspired by
the artwork of Nicolas Ruston

Edited by Ashley Stokes

UNTHANK

First Published in 2016
by Unthank Books

All Rights Reserved. A CIP record for this book is available from the British Library. Any resemblance to persons fictional or real who are living, dead or is purely coincidental.

ISBN 978-1-910061-27-5

Edited by Ashley Stokes

Book and Jacket Design by Robot Mascot
www.robotmascot.co.uk

All artworks © Nicolas Ruston 2015

Loose Ends © Tania Hershman 2016
The Slyest of Foxes © Angela Readman 2016
Coup de Grace © Ailsa Cox 2016
Perturbation © Gordon Collins 2016
Ariel © David Rose 2016
Chaconne in G Minor © Zoe Lambert 2016
But What Happens After © Jonathan Taylor 2016
Burning the Ants © Sarah Dobbs 2016
Harbour Lights © AJ Ashworth 2016
Decompression Chamber © Ashley Stokes 2016
Crow © Aiden O'Reilly 2016
Souls © Michael Crossan 2016
The Sense of an Ending © Tim Sykes 2016
All the TVs in Town © Dan Powell 2016
Nowhere Nothing Fuck-Up © UV Ray 2016

www.fifteen-endings.co.uk
www.unthankbooks.com

CONTENTS

This is The End	7
Loose Ends – Tania Hershman	15
The Slyest of Foxes – Angela Readman	25
Coup de Grace – Ailsa Cox	41
Perturbation – Gordon Collins	53
Ariel – David Rose	67
Chaconne in G Minor – Zoe Lambert	77
But What Happens After – Jonathan Taylor	89
Burning the Ants – Sarah Dobbs	99
Harbour Lights – AJ Ashworth	121
Decompression Chamber – Ashley Stokes	139
Crow – Aiden O'Reilly	169
Souls – Michael Crossan	183
The Sense of an Ending – Tim Sykes	197
All the TVs in Town – Dan Powell	209
Nowhere Nothing Fuck-Up – UV Ray	225
Authors	237

THIS IS THE END

The End Game

On the day I edited the last of the stories that make up this book, *The End: Fifteen Endings to Fifteen Paintings*, the world itself was supposed to end. Chris McCann, leader of the eBible Fellowship had proclaimed that on October 7th 2015 a great conflagration would consume the Earth. It was written in the Bible, coded into gnomic references only he could decipher. It was thus God's will. The signal of the Apocalypse, the Blood Moon had risen. It was going to happen this time, The End.

I finished reading Zoe Lambert's 'Chaconne in G Minor' and wondered if it were the last story I would ever read. I sat around and worried that the end would come before *The End*, that these stories would go unread and the paintings would be annihilated by holy fire. No one would get to play the End Game and consider how these stories had emerged from Nicolas Ruston's dark and inscrutable images.

Come midnight, the world had failed to fall apart. The End had demurred. The End blinked first, suffered a crisis of confidence. On October 8th, Chris McCann displayed all the traits of 'cognitive dissonance' that Leon Festinger describes in his 1956 book *When Prophecy Fails*. McCann promptly declared his surprise that the world was still in existence. Even so, girded rather than disabused by the disproval of his theology, he was confident that it would end 'soon'.

The End is still coming. It's always been coming. It's still out there. We are all edging towards the vanishing point, or the vanishing point is edging towards us, and it's always been this way. Always.[1]

The nature of the end – what is and what isn't, where it lies, how it plays out – is explored here in fifteen stories and the fifteen paintings that inspired them.

The Beginning of The End

The End is a project designed to produce text from image and it has an on-going relationship with the current trajectory of Nicolas Ruston's work. *The End* paintings – all of which were given as prompts to the writers – are black-and-white scratch paintings that deploy Ruston's unique process. This involves applying layers of white gloss paint to canvas before covering with an additional layer of black masonry paint. When this final layer is almost dry he scratches the surface with a surgical blade.

---

[1] The end of the world has been predicted for the years: 793, 800, 848, 1000, 1033, 1260, 1284, 1290, 1370, 1378, 1504, 1524 (twice), 1528 (twice), 1533, 1534 (twice), 1555, 1585, 1588, 1600, 1624, 1648, 1654, 1654, 1657, 1658, 1660, 1666, 1673, 1688, 1689, 1694, 1697, 1700, 1705, 1706, 1708, 1716, 1719, 1736, 1757, 1780, 1879, 1792, 1794, 1795, 1805, 1814, 1836, 1843 (three times), 1844 (twice), 1847 (twice), 1862, 1863, 1873, 1874, 1881, 1890, 1901, 1910, 1914, 1915, 1918, 1920, 1925, 1935, 1936, 1941, 1943, 1947, 1954, 1959, 1962, 1967 (twice), 1972, 1973, 1975 (the year of Nicolas Ruston's birth), 1977, 1980, 1981, 1982 (four times), 1985, 1987, 1988 (twice), 1989, 1990, 1991, 1992, 1993, 1994 (four times), 1996, 1997 (twice), 1998, 1999 (eight times), 2000 (by thirteen different groups and authorities), 2001, 2002, 2003, 2006, 2007, 2010, 2011 (four times), 2012 (twice, one of which was the so-called Mayan Apocalypse), 2013 and 2015, when the Blood Moon Prophecy vied with eBible's prediction of The End on 7th October. So, it's not just Chris McCann and it's not just us. The End has always been with us.

Some of *The End* paintings are figurative and some typographic in style. All have 'The End' emblazoned across the canvas, giving each the appearance of a final scene from a film that was never made.

Ruston is a painter and sculptor, but also an advertising creative. He is obsessed with the ways in which images, especially mass media images, bleed into and influence what we think of as our reality, the image as the whip of desire. He has exclusively worked in black and white for some time, most noticeably in his last major exhibition, *Propensity Modelling*.

Formally, *The End* represents an endpoint in Ruston's painting. He is currently returning to colour with some gusto. It's only when he looks back he will see the monochrome vistas of The End.

Propensity Modelling had no end. The final piece, 'Examining precisely the habits of who is most attuned to the commodities' secret logic' was a film loop. The film placed us in the driver's seat of a car that travelled endlessly through a ghostly landscape accompanied by an audio track of modulated birdsong, low hums and distortions. Watching it was unsettling, nauseating, like being on a ride that you desperately want to abandon even though you know it's going to go on forever ('I really like it, I feel sick,' said Ruston's agent). As Ruston told *Aesthetica* magazine, 'the image manifests as many things. We see glimpses of demons, gods, stupid looking sci-fi creatures, a few aliens, cartoon characters, weird machinery and the sublime. I'm interested in our points of reference for these images – where they come from and why'.

'Examining precisely' was surrounded by constantly reshuffled paintings, many of which resembled the sort of storyboards Ruston routinely creates in his day job, images of cars, logos and interiors. Collectively called *Dreamers who created their own nightmares*, they invited the viewer to construct their own narrative from an assemblage of images both moving and static. They have an effect, as John Peel once said of the music of The Fall, of being, 'always different, always the same.' This effect is both soothing and jarring. One of the paintings from *Propensity Modelling*, 'Faith has died science has risen' was used as the jacket image for *Unthology 4* and marked the beginning of Unthank's collaboration with Ruston.

The End develops organically from *Propensity Modelling*, but where that exhibition was diffuse in subject, themed only by what Neal Brown describes as Ruston's 'mood of soiled, corrupted beauty', *The End* has a single focus. Referencing both the graphic art of Thomas Ott and the work of Victor Burgin – who also splices image and text to provoke the viewer into creating narrative connections –*The End* is a conscious attempt by Ruston to focus on one idea rather than explore the aesthetic sensibilities behind it. It's more than a technical exercise or exploration of style. It's a system.

Propensity Modelling had no end. *The End* has fifteen that you can choose from.

The End of the Story

The process by which we produced this book harks back to the golden age of low budget exploitation filmmaking (like all good stories, ours also starts, but doesn't end, with a fortuitous encounter in one of Norwich's more salubrious public houses).

Nicolas had heard, though he wasn't sure the stories were true, that during the sixties studios would approach a screenwriter, give him a pitch, a poster and a title and send him off to write the film. These stories are not apocryphal. George Weiss, Hollywood producer of low-budget schlock hired Ed Wood to adapt the Christine Jorgensen story, giving him just a title - *I Changed My Sex* - and a poster. Wood came back with *Glen or Glenda*. Hammer supposedly indulged in the practice, too: pitch, image, get on with it writer. Between us, Nicolas and I have revived this novel approach to creative collaboration.

One night in 2012, I had just returned from a networking event that also had Nicolas Ruston in attendance, though we hadn't been introduced. I was waiting to be served in a pub and someone behind me asked the landlady, 'Do you know who Ashley Stokes is?' She said, 'He's standing there.'

This was the end of not-knowing Nicolas Ruston.

We then had a long chat about films and writing.

Nicolas says that one of the several triggers that started him along the path to creating *The End* was a line in my novel *Touching the Starfish*: 'I hate the bit at the end where everyone gets together and the loose ends are tied together and all the conflicts are wrapped up nice and simply, and everyone loves each other now.' He also liked my second book, *The Syllabus of Errors*, a series of stories that I thought of as 'all end' rather than 'all middle'. I was gloomy and frustrated when I wrote these stories. I wasn't in great shape and Nicolas has intimated that nor was he when he painted *The End* pieces. Neither of us wrote to Pamela Stephenson Connolly in *The Guardian* to ask her what we should do about it, this sense of ending.

On another night in the same pub, Nicolas told me about *The End* and asked me to write fifteen stories that used the new paintings as spurs. He wanted to see what sort of stories would emerge from images that suggested something non-specific had ended. Between us we could resurrect the 'pitch, image, get on with it' tactic from the golden age of low budget exploitation filmmaking, and take the effect achieved in Victor Burgin's work one step further. Stories wouldn't be suggested by the juxtaposition of image and text. They would be completed. We could then produce a book that would not just accompany the exhibition but become an intrinsic part of it.

Despite loving both the paintings and the collaborative aspect of the project, I only committed myself to writing one story. Far more interesting, I thought, would be to widen the base, canvas a number of responses, sound out a range of very different writers with the pitch and an image and let them get on with it. Not everyone's sense of an ending is the same, though maybe at the end of everything they will be.

Beautiful Friends

I approached fifteen writers. Some I knew from editing the *Unthology* series would likely conjure something sharp and distinct from the images. Others I'd not worked with before but I greatly admired their fictions: Tania Hershman, UV Ray, Jonathan Taylor and Zoe Lambert.

The result is a swathe of dark and human stories that wax and wane between themes of grief and death, and stories of Ragnarok and Apocalypse. The stories by Angela Readman, Ailsa Cox, Gordon Collins, David Rose, Zoe Lambert, Sarah Dobbs and AJ Ashworth fit this first, albeit broad category of grief. These stories hinge on turning points in human relationships. This isn't to say that they don't hold out their hands to the other group of stories where the end is on a different scale, the stories by Aiden O'Reilly, Michael Crossan, Tim Sykes, Dan Powell and UV Ray.

The only story to definitely fly apart from these two formations is Tania Hershman's 'Loose Ends', which is less of a story-story and more of a dramatized philosophical investigation into what is an end. This is why it heads the running order. It gets us thinking about the end. I was also keen for the vista that realizes UV Ray's 'Nowhere Nothing Fuck-Up' to be the collection's final image.

Introducing the stories in any more detail than this would be a mistake, I feel. They should speak for themselves, and in any case, I wouldn't want to give away the end.

This is Not the End

Nicolas and I have been amazed and moved by the stories the writers have composed in response to the paintings. At the very least, we hope that a few more readers will be inspired to track down their other work, all of which deserves a much wider audience.

The paintings have also been renamed, swapping their original number titles for the titles of the stories. The stories form an integral part of the exhibition. They are not an adjunct. They do not even complete the exhibition. They add a further dynamic to it, pushing the end of *The End* back further to the horizon where it belongs (who, after all, wants the end to come, apart from people like Chris McCann, and even he sees the end as a beginning that excludes people who don't take him seriously). The project is still in flux, work-in-progress. Now Nicolas has seen how the writers have responded to his End paintings, he will be producing a further series that will reply in image to each story included here. Where we go from this, I do not know. Maybe we'll commission another set of stories (*The End II, The Second Ending*). Maybe one day Nicolas and I will reach the end. For now, we are still striving.

Welcome to *The End*. It's always been coming.

Ashley Stokes
October 2015

LOOSE ENDS

TANIA HERSHMAN

The End 'Loose Ends' (2015)
Gloss and masonry paint on canvas
51 x 66cm

Lights and Tunnels

You never see it coming because you are too busy reading, or staring into the darkness or staring at the person opposite and pretending you aren't staring at the person opposite, who might be reading, or eating something, which is annoying, the eating, especially here and especially if it's noisy. When it comes, it's too bright anyway, and you reach for your sunglasses but they react oh so slowly, what's the point, and by the time, by the time. Late. It's always late. And then the person opposite is still eating, still making noise, crumpling a bag, and you and your sunglasses. You are wishing it was other, what it was before, again, although when it was that you wished for something else. Yes, you did.

Your Rope

She and he are standing, one at each. She says, Twist it, and he goes one way and she moves slightly, in a sort of dance, and they are doing it, both of them, and they are grinning, and this is, to everyone who sees, to everyone who walks past, the best possible moment, the happiest thing that a person might come across today. Just two people and a rope. Just that.

Times

You would like to think it never was and never will be can't conceive of that space and in which you and in which not you but there will be that of course because your cells your cells do not go on and on and on and so stopping and yes stopping there will be and will you feel it will you know and where is that who can say not you not you you you

Dead

- You said flowers.
- I know. I know.
- Look!
- I know. I'm ...
- It doesn't. Not now.
- Can't we just ...?
- Sorry. No. Sorry.

The Living

We decided together. The method we had developed didn't allow for any other direction. We picked the room, agreeing on each aspect. We slid our fingers down wallpapers, we slipped a hand under sofa cushions, we bent low to peer at the orientation of the pile. We, with our identical slide rules, our spirit levels, our sharp eyes and our algorithms. But when it was assembled, when we were seated finally, side by side, we knew. We tilted our heads and repositioned ourselves but there was no way to ignore it. We stood. We embraced. We whispered new plans into the air.

Run

The first time, it doesn't work, of course. All first times are alike. If it had succeeded, you would have suspected error. This is not how it is. You set it to go again. The mice do what mice do. They are interested, and then not interested, distracted by a noise in the corridor. You set it to go again. You set it to go again. And again. In the pub, later, mice are in your head and a drink is in your hand, and you are dizzy with it, all of it. You can't remember any more what it might mean to succeed, what you are even doing this for. All you know, as you wave your hand, as you attempt to get another of the same, is that tomorrow you have to set it to go again. You are sure you might remember then. Tomorrow. The mice are distracted. The mice hear a noise. You drink. You sigh. You drink again.

A Means To

It makes her anxious. And then? What if?

Wits

It is an effort to stay sharp. You find your mind has left you in between the opening of a new browser window and the carrying-out of whatever action you had planned. You stop, you look around, you wait. You find that if you wait, or distract yourself, the original plan returns. It's an oddness that seems to have arrived suddenly with the latest birthday, you are half way to four score and ten and you are disintegrating.

Yet there is something, some part of you, that thrills to this fuzziness. It is a letting go, a sinking into, a leaving to the young people that razor quality. Let them be first to shoot their hand up, you are reclining on the sofa, you may even lean to one side, you may even consider yourself Roman, reach for grapes. You stop a moment to consider what else it might mean to be Roman, to relax, to give over the fastness to our youth. Then you forget what you were thinking about. And you realise you have forgotten and you laugh at yourself, and then you enjoy the laughing at yourself and you tell yourself, possibly aloud, that this is the joy of being halfway to four score and ten. Laughing. At yourself. You are the funniest human being whose mind you inhabit. Then you turn to the computer screen, lift your fingers, mumble something that may be a prayer of gratitude for all limbs, for each heartbeat, for what it is that keeps us and keeps us. You press a key.

The Deep

Inside of one breath is another always wondering whether it might. Or might not. At the end of the pool, the lifeguard yawns and thinks about something else. Your mother and your father are thinking about you, although they do not tell you. The lifeguard is wondering if love is really. And love is wondering if the lifeguard is sincere. There is a quiz that is being written daily and only you know the answers, although there will be no questions spoken. Your mother and father have some suspicion that you are what they always hoped for, although they do not tell you. Love is giving the lifeguard another chance. The pool is giving the lifeguard one more hour. This latest breath. Yes.

Beginning of

Never start. If you start then you will finish. Sit, on your hands if necessary. Do not breathe. If you begin to breathe then you will stop. There is nothing to look at so do not turn your head. Do not wonder what might be happening elsewhere, behind you, to the side, with someone else, for someone else, in joy or in despair. Wondering leads to paths which lead to forests and, as each child knows, after the forest is only a cliff.

If you are a fool, ignore all of this. Breathe more than is recommended, use your hands for emphasis. Try a path and another path, never take a map. Rush through the forest with no torch, no spear. And when you get to the edge - you with the wild hair, the eyes that look about, the insane grin - dance. Dance without care, as if there were no edges, no falling. As if all there is is that one ripe strawberry and you cannot wait to eat.

THE SLYEST OF FOXES

ANGELA READMAN

The End 'The Slyest of Foxes' (2015)
Gloss and masonry paint on canvas
51 x 66cm

The birds decimated the seed in a day. Alice cradled her cup, blaming the pigeons muscling in for more than their share.

The shot came out of nowhere.

It was a softened sort of loud, dampened by low cloud like a pillow disguising a sob. The hedge remained motionless in the aftermath. She waited for sparrows to poke out their heads and make everything normal again before she closed the door.

It was 3pm. It couldn't be a gun. Not here, where the loudest sound was starlings and the weather was playing the log burner like a sad instrumental solo. She'd arrived knowing this, desperate to learn the sound of her breathing when her heart wasn't beating so fast. Truthfully, the quiet had unsettled her initially. People walked by so infrequently she caught herself passing mirrors and jumped. The cottage felt crowded with her creeping about, trying not to disturb the silence.

There it was again, another shot. No mistaking it. Though she'd never fired a gun in her life, she knew it. There was a distinct pause as if someone was taking a deep breath. Then the sound, putting a full stop to the stillness.

It came from somewhere behind the shed. Duck shoot. Clay pigeons. Farmers with chickens. The slyest of foxes. That had to be it, something in the area she wasn't aware of until now. She abandoned her coffee, stepped into sandals, and kicked them off. Pulling on her boots, she went outside.

The cottage could be seen from her shed. The wildflower gardens were separated by a hedge. Alice walked over the grass, worn into path by the old man's journeys to a greenhouse with his watering can. It was strange to be on someone else's property, alone. She was conscious of low windows, absent curtains, and bathrooms with unfrosted glass. Country people seemed content to step out of the shower naked and look out at the roses battling the wind. She'd never get used to that after life in the city. That lack of concern about being overlooked.

She ducked behind the fruit bushes. The currants were fruiting, between dangling pearlescent clusters, Alice could see into her neighbour's kitchen. Mr Slater sat on a pew, palms flat on the table. Opposite, was a man with a gun. He held it high, head cocked against the barrel, cooling his cheek. Mr Slater shuffled. The man raised the gun and made him sit still.

Poor Mr Slater, the quietest of men. He barely spoke to her when she moved in, no more than 'Morning' and a curt nod. She could feel him observing the wildflowers she pulled in the garden, mistaken for weeds. Feel him watching her sweat rain week after week, chopping wood to lug to the log store. He finally walked towards her waving a chainsaw.

'You can use this if you like,' he said, 'reckon it'll be quicker.'

He struggled to hand her the saw over the hedge, a straggle of blackberry snaring his sleeve. The saw was heavy. She took it, feeling its gravity, the damage it could do.

'I'm not sure I know how to use it,' she said, and a flash of her previous life flooded her. Never knowing how to do anything.

The old man slipped around to her side of the boundary to show her how to use the saw. One hand on the back. One above, shoulders raised.

'That's it, see? Nothing to it. You'll get through these logs in no time.'

It was so much quicker she wondered why he'd waited so long to show her, and immediately knew the answer. He was trying to decide if she was serious about country living. He didn't think she'd still be here in the winter. No one did.

The day she returned the saw, she found him hacking back branches, creating a path.

'Thought it might be useful,' he said, 'if you want to borrow something again.' He pushed aside a branch. It sprung back, whipping his chest. He worked on, refusing to feel it. She couldn't help but be slightly moved, at this gap, just for her. For some people the smallest of allowances are huge, she knew.

The man with the gun looked out of the patio doors. Alice froze, waiting for his gaze to slide over her. He stood still for sometime and turned sharply towards Mr Slater, coughing, head bowed as a schoolboy afraid of shooting his headmaster the wrong look. She ran, crouched low.

The strip in the hedge was slightly overgrown now that she had her own chainsaw. It was just enough for a slight person to pass through. She locked her door and paced the kitchen, dirt forking off her boots onto the tiles. There was no phone in the cottage. Idiot move. She loved the simplicity of it when she arrived. Her friends all had children. Over the years, she stopped being able to call without feeling like something to add to a list of Things I Must Do Today. Friends of His she left behind with a few clothes, books, and CD's she couldn't stand listening to anymore.

There was a phone in the pub several miles away. How long was the walk? Too long. She dragged her mobile out of the breadbin, plugged in the charger and met its dead eye. Nothing. No surprise. It was placed in the bin the day she arrived. She had allowed His messages to echo and die. Retrieving it, the phone refused to come on, as if it had given up believing she'd ever talk to anyone.

The TV in the lounge was surrounded by boxes. Alice switched it on and flicked. There he was. The gunman. The picture had been taken in July. Streaks of sunlight and shadow lay a pattern across his plain lemon shirt. He was clean-shaven, almost glowing in the photo. His face looked like he'd just stepped out of the shower and his skin was sensitive to soap. Alice knelt on the floor, so close to the screen when she breathed she left a smudge on the man's mouth. His name was Mark White.

'Following the dispute with a former girlfriend, Sarah Williams on Tuesday, Mr White was last seen driving north.'

Two people were shot. One was dead. The other in surgery. Alice pulled her legs out from under her and got up, unable to feel her feet.

She didn't decide what to do next. She didn't decide to go to her kitchen, open the cupboard and grab a jar of marmalade. There was no plan to stare into the freezer, pull out a small loaf of bread and sit it on the Aga. She did so like a woman who smiles when she's nervous, or is compelled to put on the kettle if someone died. The carrots in the fridge needed using. Alice peeled and chopped, fried onions and shredded herbs with her fingers.

The soup simmered; islands of coriander drifted on an orange sea. She recalled the man standing by the window like a child with a toy he was bored with, scratching his face along the cool steel, bristles worrying his skin. She grabbed an electric razor and a towel from the bathroom, placed them in a wicker basket and sat the food on top. Both hands gripping the handle, she slipped through the hedge.

He'd see her before she got there, carrying no weapons but soup. He'd see her stupid purple dress, sunburnt shoulders, and the biker boots that didn't match. He would see and decide whether to shoot her on sight.

She approached slowly, uncertain if she was a brave woman or one set on suicide. The gunman had been on the run over twenty-four hours. Twenty-four hours of looking over his shoulder, clutching a shotgun, stomach growling, inconvenient, ignored. He had to be starving. Alice justified her actions while acknowledging that reason had nothing to do with it. She was a woman who simply never knew what to do but serve food.

Chicken and rosemary, filo pastry stuffed with goat cheese and mint, biscotti and fresh coffee like an apology perched on His desk, cold before anyone noticed it was there. Throughout her marriage, she plated up solace when her husband came in from work. It was a reflex to open a bottle of red, let it breathe, if he'd had a difficult client, or someone was parked in front of the garage. This was her art, if she had one, appeasement. She offered it as quietly as a keeper afraid of waking a sleeping bear.

There was no point in knocking. The gunman saw her on the crazy paving, hands filled with the basket. Head full of: This was a stupid idea. Turn back. He hid the gun behind his back childishly. Alice could see it between his legs. Pretend to know nothing; it felt true.

The patio door opened a slither. The man stared at her.

'Who are you? What do you want? What have you got?'

He had lost all pretence of manners. Everything was cut to the bone. Alice looked at his face, slightly puffy under his stubble. Scratched raw. She was neither old enough to be his mother, nor young enough for him to approach her in a bar. The stubble on his chin was redder than the hair on his head. The late afternoon caught each bristle like sandpaper pressed to a match.

'I sometimes bring Mr Slater food,' she said, 'since his wife passed away.'

She looked into the kitchen at the old man, still alive, shaking his head. The flask squeaked as she unscrewed the lid, soup steamed a small cloud onto the window.

The man sniffed and swallowed his spit.

'I'm ... his son,' he said, 'just visiting for a bit.'

'There's plenty of food, enough for you both, if you're hungry?'

She hoped she was smiling; she wasn't convinced. She smiled for her life. The gunman opened the door and she stepped into the kitchen, ignoring the gun, pretending to be deaf to Mr Slater's protests.

'I don't need anything today,' he said, 'seriously, get yourself away.'

She sat the basket on the table and pulled three bowls off the dresser. The spoons rattled around in a jug on the counter. She placed one beside Mr Slater, and one opposite the pew. The man sat, gun leaning against his chair. Alice sliced the bread and poured soup. He sniffed it, waiting for her to swallow something first. She sat, and blew on her spoon, forcing the liquid to glide down her throat.

Mr Slater didn't move. 'You should make a move. You must have plenty to do.'

'I have plenty of time.' She hoped it was true.

The gunman dipped a crust into the soup and ate, clearing the bowl. He looked almost shy, eyeing Mr Slater's food.

'Are you eating that?' he asked, scratching his jaw.

The skin reddened, itching for a shave. No matter what a man did Alice always felt slightly sorry for him seeing him shave, sudded and shirtless in front of the mirror. Dots of red rising, blotted on paper, so much blood so close to the surface.

Mr Slater pushed the bowl across the table, carrot lapping over the sides.

'Take it,' he said. 'Take whatever you like and just go.'

'Is that any way to speak to your loving son?'

The man glared. His eyes were blue as a faded willow pattern plate.

Alice surveyed the room. There was a kitbag on the floor by the fridge. Black. Canvas. His. It was the sort of room where nothing seemed to be put away. It was all out on display, the crockery slotted onto oak dressers, glass jars nudging one another on the shelves. The door to the lounge was ajar. Through it, she could see the grandfather clock. The case had been shot, killing the notion of passing time. The wall was peppered with holes; broken glass pebbled the carpet. Next to the clock was the phone. She got up.

'Where are you going?' His fingers curled around the gun.

'Just clearing the table.' She paused, gripping the bowls, just feet away from the phone. He was rummaging in the basket, still ravenous. He brought out the marmalade and delved to the bottom to see if she'd brought more food.

'What's this?' He inspected the razor. 'Why did you bring this?'

'Oh, I just brought it for Mr Slater,' she said. 'He broke his.'

They both looked at Mr Slater's long beard the colour of pepper.

'Bullshit! You know, don't you? You're full of it!' The gun lifted. 'Who sent you? The police? What …? They thought if they sent some daft bitch in a hippie dress I'd just turn myself in or something?'

'I came on my own. I haven't spoken to the police.' She regretted saying it instantly. Should have said she had called. They were on their way. It would make sense to run. Now.

He pointed to the pew with the gun. 'Sit there, don't move.'

She sat beside Mr Slater, the gun on her chest, the eyes of the man holding it all over her face. She knew what he saw. He saw a slow moving creature who had stopped caring about things like haircuts and fashion. It didn't matter what she wore in the country, nobody saw. Except him. He saw everything.

'There's no need to drag anyone else into it,' Mr Slater said. 'You assumed the cottage was empty. There's no harm done. You came, you ate, now you can leave. There's a Morris Minor in the garage I haven't driven for years. Take it.'

'Just shut up for a minute, I have to think.'

Mark White scratched his chin on his shoulder, deciding what to do. One minute passed.

Ten.

They were still silently waiting after an hour.

The gun dipped, rose, and fell, as if his arms ached holding it.

'I need the bathroom,' Mr Slater said.

'You'll have to wait.'

'I can't wait, not at my age'

'I need to go, too,' Alice said.

She could see him picturing the pair pissing where they sat, and considering the bathroom, just off the utility. One door away. Alice straightened. He stroked her sternum with the gun.

'Hold his hand and stand up.'

Mr Slater's hand was cold squeezing hers. They shuffled to the bathroom as one, ushered by the gun at her spine. One after the other, he allowed them inside. Mr Slater went first. Outside, she could hear water fall.

'Don't lock the door,' he called. 'Try anything and I'll shoot you both, starting with her.'

They sat at the table once more. Mr Slater propped his head on his hand, closed his eyes and began to doze off. It was starting to get dark, dusk sloped into the room and spread out on the rug. The oblong of light from the window closed on the wall.

'Thank you for letting us go to the bathroom,' Alice said. 'It was decent of you.'

'I am decent, whatever they're saying.' There was actual blood on his neck now. He scratched at a fleck.

She didn't reply. Plenty of decent men do bad things, and plenty of bad ones wear a suit of decency. She could never tell which was which.

'I didn't go there intending to shoot her. I just wanted her to hear my side of the story. That's why I took the gun, so she'd listen. I didn't know she'd met someone and he'd be there. I didn't want to kill her. I never did.'

He looked so tired, other than when he spoke. His agitation over faded arguments seemed to be the only thing keeping him awake.

'She's not dead,' Alice said. 'I saw on the news. They're operating …You could turn yourself in, explain it was an accident. It will be better for you, than if they have to find you.'

She wasn't sure that he heard. His eyelids drooped heavily over the gun. They closed, and she shifted an inch in her seat. He shook awake like a dog on a chain dreaming of rabbits and hills.

Mr Slater slept. Throughout the night, it seemed he might never wake, and she might never really sleep again. The other man's eyes closed for seconds at a time. He bolted upright whenever she moved.

'I want to see her, say I'm sorry,' he said. 'Tell her I love her. She might forgive me. Eventually, she'll forget.'

Alice was unsure if he was speaking to her. For hours now, he seemed to be speaking to himself like a child looking for something to make everything OK.

'She'll never forget,' Alice said. If these were her last words they'd be clear. 'Even if she loves you, and forgives, once she's seen another side of you it's never the same. I was like that with my husband, Michael. Everything looked perfect. I cooked, cleaned, kissed him and smiled all our photos in France, but I'd stopped being myself years ago. You can apologise to a woman all you like, but no apology can change that. You will never be the same man to her. Nothing changes that.'

It surprised her to speak of her husband, so frankly, to use the name she had avoided thinking for so long. It held no power over her. If she died now she'd die honestly, she had said what had to be said. It was done.

The man bowed his head, slowly nodded, and looked up. The sun was starting to rise. They saw it slot between the hills beyond the garden and slip across the patio, the shrubs in the pots losing their grip of the dark. He stood up with the gun. There was no going back, and nowhere to run. There was nothing but now.

The air was cool, drifting into the kitchen it carried in scraps of birdsong as he slid open the door. He wandered outside and stood still for some time, looking up at the hills in the distance. Alice locked the door and began to walk to the phone. Mr Slater woke with a start. She stopped and looked towards the sound outside with him. One shot, clear as a full stop puncturing the sunrise.

COUP DE GRACE

AILSA COX

The End 'Coup de Grace' (2015)
Gloss and masonry paint on canvas
51 x 66cm

We can't take Freddie with us, not this time. Those days of skittering over the beach, yapping and frolicking – those days are gone forever. Jeff said when he went for the papers this morning, Fred just lay down on the pavement a few steps from the house, before they'd even reached the corner, as if he hadn't got the strength to carry on. He seemed perky enough, when we first arrived, fetching his ball from the back of the sofa, dropping it expectantly for the kids to throw. But poor old Freddie, it can't be long now. That wheezy cough – I always thought it was a fur ball or too much excitement, with the kids running round him screaming their heads off – now it's almost constant – and he lumbers up the stairs one by one – that old jack-in-the-box frenzy, all of it, gone.

Evelyn's got her old typewriter out, what a novelty she says – Sally clacking away at her machine like something out of *Mad Men*, Toby fretting for his turn – words that go straight on the paper! Once Toby said to Evelyn, 'Grannie, when you die, can I look after Fred and Little Cat?' I said that wouldn't happen for a long time yet, he'd be grown up, but Evelyn just laughed, *I'm ninety-three my dear, I can't go on forever.* As it turned out, Little Cat went under the wheels of a taxi, and what's left of him lies buried in the garden, close to the grave of the long-deceased Big Cat.

I can't go on forever. But she does. For as long as I've known my mother-in-law, she's been the same brisk elderly widow, her voice as clear and commanding as a Shakespearean actress. 'Just what he needs, a good woman taking charge. It was all his fault his first marriage broke up. He was dreadful in those days, a real chauvinist pig. He never did anything with the children.'

If that was ever true, it's different with his second family. It's my husband who takes charge of the expedition, squeezing the five of us into the car, remembering not to forget binoculars. He explains carefully to the kids what it is we're going to see, it's a very special day because the three big ships are in Liverpool at the same time, and they're all going to pass one another, and it's called the Three Queens, because each ship is called after a Queen, Mary, Elizabeth, and what's the other one? Yes, that's right, *Victoria*.

A dazzling day, glittering with the promise of summer to come. At Waterloo, clusters of human figures are heading for the sea, like Hebrews on the shores of Galilee. We've missed the climax of the three ocean liners greeting one another, in some kind of quadrille, but it doesn't matter too much, we can still see the giant ships back in port, hazy as ghosts in the distance, and we can discern movement, they're coming back again, making their slow and ceremonious departure. Evelyn asks to be taken back to the car. I watch the two of them progressing across the sand, the tiny woman wrapped up in her bulky beige coat, leaning against her big bear of a son. No little dog shepherding them along, not ever again, no snapping of fingers, *come on, Freddie boy*.

Fred is ancient in dog years, nearly eighteen, the last in a long line of feisty terriers – and the final connection with my father-in-law, who I never met, who's just a blue-bleached figure among the fading photographs in Evelyn's living room, showing off a puppy Evelyn says is Freddie, though I privately think not, Evelyn's hair being blonder, her face just as determined, but somehow more open, the face of a woman still in her prime. How many years have we been coming to this beach? That Christmas – Sally must have been a toddler – was I pregnant with Toby? – the coldest place in England, the ribbed lines of sands rigid under their dusting of snow, boots crunching in the salty patches of ice left by the tide.

Sally pirouettes on the sands, practicing her dance routine – soon she'll be as tall as Evelyn – then as tall as I am. Through the binoculars you can make out the ships inching almost imperceptibly from port. Toby wants the toilet so we walk up in search of somewhere, and then we have to buy ice creams, and just as we're leaving the cafe, a cruise liner glides past, like a hallucination, like a flat from a West End musical, and Sally says wistfully, 'I wish that Fred was here.'

The kids like the ships, but not as much as the typewriter. It takes quite a lot of effort to make the keys hit the paper, the metal claws tangling and sticking until you get used to the right amount of pressure.

'Do you remember those golfball typewriters?' says Jeff, 'used to be like a circular thing?'

'I've never used a typewriter.'

'You must have done. What about when you were a student?'

'No. I had a word processor.'

'That's a typewriter.'

'No it isn't.'

'Before her time,' says Evelyn, but he's already googling 'typewriters 1990s', determined to prove that my own memories are misleading.

The vet is a sensible, middle-aged Scot, and her verdict is swift. 'I think we've reached the end now. It's time to let him go.'

'Are you sure?' says Jeff, 'he was playing in the park ... He seemed not so bad ...'

'They try to please you,' she says. 'They try so hard.'

We thought we were here to up Fred's medication. Trying to help, we've inadvertently sentenced him to death. Fred's heart is failing, his lungs filling with fluid and his other organs distorting under the pressure. A few more weeks are left to him at most – it's better to act, she says, for us to act, for Fred's sake and most of all for Evelyn's.

We discuss arrangements, make a plan – how can we still be doing this, driving back to Evelyn's with Fred himself, the corpse-to-be, lying on the back seat with the shopping? All I can say is, 'Evelyn's pretty sensible', and Jeff says, 'He was getting too much for her. I was going to suggest we take him back with us.'

'Were you?'

'She'd have said no. But I was going to make the suggestion.'

The cold wind has blown the promise of summer away. By the time we pull in, the rain's coming down like molten glass.

'My darling boy,' says Evelyn, 'dear old Freddie. Oh no, surely not, these vets, you know.' She gives out the laugh that is one of her characteristics, short and gruff. 'They can't wait for the *coup de grace*, they're like, oh, what's his name ...'

'Harold Shipman?' I say.

'Wasn't that awful? And they all liked him! They thought he was a good doctor.'

'You trust that vet,' Jeff reminds her. 'You've always said how good she is.' As Jeff lays out the plan, she listens in silence, completely in his hands. The vet can come to the house on Friday. We'll take the kids to Jeff's daughter's house in Manchester on Thursday – they've been agitating for a sleepover with her two – and then we'll all meet there for lunch on Saturday, before the long drive home.

'You don't need to be here Ma,' he says. 'You can both go into Liverpool, have a cup of tea somewhere. Leave it to me, I'll take care of things.'

Suddenly my eyes fill my tears.

'Don't,' he says, 'don't.'

His eyes are wet too. Only Evelyn's are dry, but she's quiet for a moment, straightening invisible creases on her skirt.

What will we tell the children? The question was the first we asked ourselves, on the way back from the vet's. We'll tell them next week, at home, once they've settled down at school. We won't tell them everything. We'll tell them Fred died in his sleep. That won't be a lie, exactly, though it won't be exactly the truth.

Jeff's father died in his sleep. After he retired he'd always bring her a cup of tea in the morning. If she woke up first – as she usually did, she says, with that truncated laugh of hers – she'd pretend to be asleep; it gave him so much pleasure. In this story – one she tells not often, but always word for word – she lie there unawares, until the sun comes up, until the very moment Fred is pulling at the bedclothes. But don't you know when something's dead, don't you sense it right away, just as you can tell when some one isn't really sleeping?

I can hear Freddie padding around at night, with his wheezy old man's cough, and when the spasm stops I hope and fear that this might be the end. Every morning, I make sure I'm up even earlier than the children. I don't want them to be the ones to find him. I sleep lightly and dream deeply in the hours before waking. I dream there's a mewing at the kitchen window, a feline shape, amazing, how weird, another tortoiseshell, with the exact same markings as poor old Little Cat. But her face isn't as pretty, the head weirdly blunt and squarish. I dream that we're having another baby, and I'm glad, except it's not me that's pregnant, it's Jeff, and I can't help feeling that fifty-seven seems risky for a primagravida.

Sally reminds us when Freddie's due to takes his pill, and she wraps it up in a little piece of ham to give to him. She's a good girl, considerate and decorous whenever we visit Evelyn. They are both good children, curled up on the sofa next to Fred, Sally in her dressing gown, Toby in his dinosaur onesie. These days drag by, the last days of Freddie, and I wonder if Evelyn feels the same mad grief scrabbling inside her. I wonder how it felt to find her husband's body. I wonder how she learnt to keep her self-control.

Because I find self-control extremely difficult. I'd do anything to be home. I wish we'd finished Freddie then and there, the day we saw the vet. I wish it were over. I can't stand to look at his hopeful, trusting face, and yet I want to hold onto him, the beating heart beneath the rough white fur. The sheets of typing are littered on Evelyn's carpet:

> *Dear Fred,*
> *you aare the best dog in the world. get wellsoon. love Sally and toby.*

XXXXXXXXXXXXXXXXXXXXXXXXXXXXXX

He is just a dog. I don't even like dogs especially, I'm not an animal person, and yet and yet and yet ...

What will we tell the children?

I dream I'm scouring Evelyn's bathtub, removing so much of the enamel it leaves great black patches, like wounds.

I have, in fact, been cleaning the bathroom, and sweeping at cobwebs invisible to Evelyn's failing eyes. I've been bleaching coffee mugs ringed with stains and vacuuming hairs from the sofa, while Jeff fixes the fence and retunes the telly and has a go at the leak in the roof. 'How is he,' Evelyn asks, 'how's my boy, is he over that trouble?'

Fine, I tell her, Jeff's back to his old self, and she takes me at my word, or seems to. What I don't say is I wish we weren't here. We could have had a holiday, I wish he'd take it easy, but we're here for reassurance, and that's why Jeff insists on going up a ladder, with me holding on for dear life.

'Could you do something, for me darling?' she says, handing me a brown envelope, faintly smelling of damp, with something bulging inside, a cassette. 'This is for my send-off. Nothing gloomy, darling. A little bit of Mozart, nothing too heavy, and Frank Sinatra, he had such a wonderful voice. "Come Fly With Me", I thought it might raise a bit of a smile ... darling, could you make another copy, just to be on the safe side? I'm not going to ask Jeff because I want it to be a surprise. There's a song in there he used to love when he was little, we used to sing it in the car, do you know the one, *Little Boxes, little boxes, and they all look just the same* ...'

At the end we're all there, the three of us together – Evelyn for Fred, and Jeff for his mother, and me for my husband, the love of my life. Jeff dug a grave next to Little Cat and Big Cat while I drove Evelyn and Fred to the park for one last time. Evelyn watched from the park bench as Fred played with another dog, no longer himself, and yet fully alive. We were told some time before lunch, but no sooner have we put the kettle on than the phone rings to tell us the vet is on her way, and Fred's remaining hours have shrunk to minutes and soon they will be no more than seconds.

'Don't,' says Jeff again, 'don't. You'll frighten him.'

Ever since the verdict, the tears have been brimming over. I was relieved when my period came because I could blame my hormones. Evelyn's been patting at her eyes with a handkerchief a little more than she usually does but I'm the one who has to go to the bathroom and rinse my face. I don't understand it. I never cried this much when Jeff was rushed into hospital.

We spread a red velvet curtain on the sofa, where Fred would always leap up to see who was coming. Jeff settles him down there, with his head on Evelyn's lap, and she fondles his ears. 'My darling boy,' she murmurs, 'my brave little Freddie. Oh my darling boy, my dearest, my Freddie, my brave little boy …'

We position ourselves, Jeff next to his mother, me crouching on the carpet, still thick with Freddie's hairs. Jeff's father watches from the photo on the sideboard, amongst all the pictures of the family, in sepia and black and white and colour. Carefully, almost lovingly, the vet shaves Fred for the injection, revealing pale skin that's nearly human. Evelyn's voice runs on, *my darling*, and a howl breaks from Jeff. I keep looking in Fred's eyes, dark and unchanging.

I save the fur, keeping it safe in my pocket.

PERTURBATION

GORDON COLLINS

The End 'Perturbation' (2015)
Gloss and masonry paint on canvas
51 x 66cm

The wires between the pylons have snapped and thrash around sparking on the raindrops. Beneath is the wreck of a helicopter. There is crumpled metal mixed with earth. A ladder is poking through the smashed window and lies on the shoulder of the pilot's body. Another ladder is broken in two next to it and a third ladder lies further away. Water gushes out of a blocked gutter on the nearby cottage. A girl in a pink raincoat lies on the ground shouting. A man comes out of the cottage towards her.

An hour before this, that man was in the cottage, standing over the washing-up and looking across the fields at the pylons. He viewed the scene through the eyes of a mathematician, extracting the symbols from it until it was a diagram. He visualised a pipeline of electromagnetic field surrounding the wires – a tube of small arrows flowing around it. He wondered how a passing raindrop would interact with it. He thought of it hitting the wires between the pylons, instantly evaporating and causing only a slight perturbation. Then he thought of different configurations of raindrops, for, in the quasi-infinite deluge, there must exist pyramids, spheres, pulsing shards and any geometry imaginable. Could a freak configuration react with the field to amplify the perturbations and accumulate into an electromagnetic wave? Could this wave reach the cottage?

He saw Jude return from school in her pink raincoat with her high-vis vest over it. Her smiling face peaked out from the hood. She didn't come straight in, though, but looked up at the side of the cottage with concern. She came to the back door, opened it and shouted, 'Dad, where's the ladder?'

'In the garage, why?'

'The gutter's blocked. I'm going to fix it.'

'Wait! You can't –'

The door slammed and a moment later she was running out, past the kitchen window to the garage.

The obvious worry was a tall ladder under the pylon wires. But he knew that the regulations required the wires to be higher than the tallest ladder and his ladder, even at full extension, was only an average height. More worrying was a fall from the ladder – year after year falls were the number one accidental killer. Falls were an accident category that he needed to be targeting. At her age, disease and illness were of far less concern. She was not susceptible to self-harm. She was healthy in both mind and body and so, apart from the statistical outlier of brain tumours, that left accidents. He had done everything he could to protect her against traffic – insisting on high-vis clothing and selecting her walking routes and times to minimise the mean maximum car speed metric. That left household accidents of which the greatest killers were falls 23%, accidental poisoning 15%, strangulation 7%, suffocation 4% and electricity 3%.

But the figures didn't tell the whole story. Once he had completed his risk analysis, he came to the realisation that the number one killer of teenage girls, worse than falls, self-harm and traffic, was unforeseen circumstance. More specifically unforeseen combinations of those accidents listed in the most common causes of home deaths. Fate does not paint in monochrome but chooses from the palate of risk: alcohol and bicycles, the razor blade and the polished floor, the plastic bag and the blind cord, the power tool, the stepladder and the dog. Hair dryers and baths are a foreseeable catastrophe and so rarely mixed. Curling tongs and sinks kill more. He was sure of it. Only suicidals will succumb to a hairdryer in a bath but an unthinking teenager may easily find herself using an extension cord to crimp in front of the bathroom mirror, if, say the bedroom mirror is occupied by a unconscientious parent.

He put on his raincoat and rushed out after her across the lawn under the crackling pylon wires and into the garage. He could hear the helicopter in the distance, quieter than before. In the garage, the ladder was in three sections each painted in fluorescent green. He watched her take each section down off the wall and lay them on the floor. She had schoolwork to do and she had a violin recital tomorrow and yet she still found the energy to clean the gutters.

'You will be careful, won't you?' he said and regretted it for he knew that this sort of general warning only transferred his own anxieties. It only served to show mistrust and reinforce a paternalistic fallacy, pretending to take responsibility for the project, disempowering her, enticing her into transgression.

'Specifically I am worried about the combination of a slippery ladder and the high voltage electricity,' he said.

'The ladder can't reach the pylons, can it?'

'No. That isn't my worry.'

'What is?'

'I don't know. I suppose it's more the slippery ladder.'

'OK. You can hold it at the bottom. These shoes have a lot of tread on them. Look.' She put her foot on a ladder rung and pulled it back. There was no way it could have slipped.

'OK. Good,' he said.

She had always been respectful of but not restricted by his fears. They spent hours together assessing the risks of a sleepover or a school trip to a local nature reserve. Still she found a way to accommodate his paranoia while not allowing it to overwhelm her own mind. She was devoted to her music and her studies, which progressed towards top grades, although he would never know it. At dinnertime she had to regulate her conversation for fear of provoking his anxieties. For him, literature increased the likelihood of suicide. Mathematics was the route to madness.

Economics – an overarching concern. But Biology was a necessity and so was chemistry where it pertained to biology or medicine. It paid to have a working knowledge of bites, infections and poisons and their antidote and avoidance. Psychology too. She had begun to understand how fear works. The force of the death drive. How it spiralled around death and will not speak of it except to show us the signs of death, if you were sensitive enough to read them.

The sound of the helicopter grew louder again as if it were circling. There was an airport nearby but they did not usually fly over the cottage. The lines buzzed louder in the wet as the moisture aided the ionization of the air around the wires. He did not help her take the ladder sections out but watched her carefully back each one around the corner of the garage, over the top of the Ford Fiesta, which had not been driven for four months, and out onto the lawn. He winced as she came under the pylons even though he could see the clearance was over ten metres. This was not the worry, he told himself. It was the flagship risk that other risks sailed behind. The water gushed out of the drain. The grass was slippery. The whole scene became more dreadful, he thought. A contemporary Turner would have tied himself to a pylon in order to understand it. Even though she couldn't have thrown the ladder that high. The strongest wind could not have blown it that high. No bird –

'Dad!'

'Yes.'

'Watch out?'

'What?'

'Watch out. You'll trip on the ladders.'

'Yes. I'm watching.'

The buzzing and the rain beating on the roof made it hard to hear her. She lay the three sections out on the lawn in parallel like the Roman numeral for three. They looked up at the gutter on the corner of the cottage. It spluttered out rain, drenching the corner of the cottage. Despite his mathematical achievements which, although they were far from the stuff that gets one prizes or professorships, had been recognised by the few still working in K-theory as significant theorems that may never have been uncovered if not for him, despite this, he had often thought himself inadequate in that he could not apply such learning and that, while some men could build or arrange the building of complicated information systems or great lines of pylons, he, with all his understanding of the materials and the flow of water, could not fix his gutters. A few years ago, he had been up there himself and fitted a cover but, evidently, this had not been sufficient. The last time this had happened, it had leaked into Jude's bedroom and caused a damp patch, which gave a home to the mould Stachybotrys chartarum and its spores, which she had inhaled for a month before he noticed. Spores that had infected her lungs and likely damaged her immune system. Spores that could have killed if he had not moved her into the spare room for three months while he treated and dried out the room. He would have to move her out tonight, he thought, but then realised that the mould could not grow so quickly and that there were untested electrical items in the spare room.

He looked up at the wall. The top of the ladder would perch firmly against the bricks which would provide ample friction even if wet. The bottom would be on the wet soil, digging in and immovable. She would be able to hold the ladder at the top. The gutters did not protrude unduly and so she would easily be able to reach over and clean out what leaves she could and, from the look of it and his previous experience, just clearing a few leaves would breach the dam and the others would flow out behind them.

'Just pull the leaves out and I'll fix it properly later.'
'OK.'
'Did you check your pockets?'
'Yes.'
'Just throw the leaves on the ground. I'll clear them up.'
'OK. Don't slip on them.'

'I'll clear them up when they're dry.'
'OK.'

The clouds grew darker. Lightning struck and thunder came five seconds later. He could see the helicopter. The pylons strode across the field as if they were giants stuck in the mud held together by ropes to keep them from losing each other. He tried to analyse the scene as if reading a page of mathematics. He knew that the symbolic world could be as dangerous as the real. He had compiled his own list of symbolic killers: mislabelled poisons, misidentified mushrooms, badly written appliance instructions, plugs wired with the wrong colours and twisted road signs like the 'No Entry' sign he had once seen on a slip road, which appeared to admit cars to travel the wrong way on the motorway. But a career of manipulating symbols had left him no closer to the mystery behind them. Not that he could ever believe in an extra-human intelligence. These signs came from man not God. But there was something inexplicable about the way society, the 'Big Other', spoke to us. There was something going on, between man and his symbols that could not be explained. There was something in the way they had organised themselves and taken us hostage that gave the symbolic a power that it should not have had on its own.

It whirred around his head: a roman three, the rhythm of rain interfering with the helicopter's, the pylons, the various coefficients of friction involved. He tried to 'see out' the picture so that he could just see the symbols. What was it saying? Was it an equation, a theorem or just a calculation? The buzzing wires. Jude. He couldn't compute it all.

'Jude, I don't like it. There are too many variables. Anything can happen.'

'OK. You go in. I'll be in in a minute.'

'You come too. Please, Jude. We can fix it tomorrow.'

'What?'

'Come in.' He went to her.

'Dad!'

His foot caught in a cell of the middle ladder section and he fell. She helped him up and brought him inside. He wasn't badly hurt. It was just the markings of a fall and not a broken bone. The helicopter was nearer but quieter. She sat him on the sofa and fetched towels and a plaster. She turned on the standard lamp and brought his book. She brought soup, bread and some cheeses. They laughed about his fall.

She stood. 'I'll just clear up outside,' she said and she kissed him on the head.

'Do it tomorrow.'

'The wall will get soaked. They say it's going to get worse tomorrow.'

'At least it will be light and I'll be able to help.'

'OK, I'll just close the garage door.'

She went out. The helicopter was lower. The section of ladder he had tripped on had swivelled around ninety degrees to form an 'H' with the other two sections. The tired helicopter pilot picked it out in the poor visibility. He saw a bright 'H' in an open space. He saw someone in a high-vis vest approaching. He did not see the grey pylons. He decided this was the landing pad.

The accident damaged Jude's spinal cord and she was unable to walk again. They obtained a disability grant, which paid for the cottage to be fitted with the necessary ramps and railings and for certain doors to be widened to accommodate her wheelchair. She moved downstairs into the dining room away from the damp and her father. For a while, their finances were perilous, relying as they did on his pension and his few tutoring jobs. But then Jude persuaded her father to accept visitors: one or two school friends and some of the ladies from the village including the mother of the pilot who had died on their lawn. These friendships sustained her until she was able to adapt to her circumstances. They set up an office in her room and from there she was able to run a business trading reclaimed building materials. Soon she was able to pay back the disability grant and could hire a carer who spent more and more time looking after her father as she became abler and he degenerated. Eventually he succumbed to a combination of drink and heart failure and not, as she had feared, to the fall down the cottage's steep stairwell that had contributed to the death of her mother many years before.

ARIEL
DAVID ROSE

The End 'Ariel' (2015)
Gloss and masonry paint on canvas
51 x 66cm

Cross-hatching of branches against the sky; a Beatles song warping the urban night ... How little it takes to conjure his shade, dissolve the years.

I hear his whistling in the washroom echo the tune I didn't then know. I lagged behind in everything.
It was 1965, my first job. I was sixteen, spotty and shy. He was ... I never knew how old Keith was. Thinking back, he couldn't have been so very much older – three years, four, maybe more. But he was a world ahead. He was part of the adult world I was sidling into; he was what I aspired to be. Even his spots were swarthily sophisticated.
I apprenticed myself to him: his way of knotting his tie, of leaving his collar-button undone, the way he draped his jacket, matador-like, across his arm – I took careful note. How I envied his accent, his easy adenoidal, "Roight, wack!" We all affected Liverpudlian accents in those days, but ours were ersatz; his, I knew, was the real thing, his living in Slough a temporary aberration – he couldn't have been born there.
It was hard work keeping up. I had just mastered the tie and saved up for the Chelsea boots when he soared ahead again – into leathers, zipped boots and helmet: he had bought a motor-bike. It changed our lives.
A white Ariel it was, its distinctive front forks the classiest thing I had seen. It would be there when I arrived in the mornings, parked beside the bike-shed, still quivering. I would lay my hands lovingly on the petrol-tank, squeeze the brake-lever and dream. At five o'clock, I would watch him donning

his jacket, zipping himself in while I held his gauntlets, squire to his leather-clad knighthood. Following him down the stairs, I would listen enviously to the click of steel-shod boots.

Then, while he mounted and spurred the Ariel, I would pedal off frantically to reach the road, knowing he would roar up behind me, throttle down, and with a hand on my shoulder, propel me along until, at the roundabout, with a shouted, 'Roight, wack, see yer tomorrer,' he would roar off, leaving me prey to inertia.

One day, I let down my back tyre, pretending a puncture, hoping desperately that he would offer a lift on his pillion. He offered to mend the puncture. 'Looks like a dodgy valve,' he said with an expert glance, and slid on his gauntlets. I was glad, though, afterwards. Something would have subtly changed between us. How could Pegasus have a pillion rider? My place was still pedalling forlornly behind. Besides, I would have a bike of my own one day – I was already saving. Not a white one, though, not straight off. I would graduate to that.

Something did change, that summer, but in a different way: Keith bought another bike - a Thruxton 500cc – a racing job, and a battered van, transporter-cum-workshop. I felt then that I would never catch up.

Weekends he raced at Brands Hatch. Monday mornings I would be caught up in his cloud of esteem, sitting on his desk as he relayed the race to the Accounts Department. One race in particular stands in my mind. As the flag went down, he couldn't get started; he had to run and push, the engine turning just as the leaders caught him up. He joined them, edging into the pack. At the finish, he was placed third. Nobody realised he was one lap behind. In my eyes, that put him indisputably first, his mocking insouciance worth any number of hollow legitimate wins.

I was settling into work by this time, with gumption enough to enter the typing pool alone, to flirt, even, with the post-girl, secure in Keith's patronage. Suddenly, his hand was removed.

With a cheery wave and a 'Roight, wack, be seein' yer,' he left the firm.

Looking back, I realise that was just what I needed. My apprenticeship was finished. After the initial inertia, I picked up speed on my own account. I would slip off my cycle-clips and click up the stairs, jacket coolly draped over one arm. I would whistle *'Eleanor Rigby'* in the washroom. There were school-leavers to impress, typists to take out. My confidence, though feigned, was effective. I knew I would always be one lap behind, but no one seemed to notice

I was still saving hard. Eventually, I did it – my own motorbike. Not an Ariel, but a Triumph Tiger Cub. Still, it was a start. Nobody rubbed neatsfoot oil into leather with such voluptuous pride as I.

I commandeered Keith's parking space by the bike-shed, my oil-drip mingling with his on the asphalt – we were now blood brothers. At five, I would click down the stairs, wink at the juniors, and with practised nonchalance, kick up the prop-stand and swing astride.

I was now fully fledged. My spots had dried up, my confidence increased to the point where I now carried a spare helmet and offered pillion rides to typists. One of them accepted. She would giggle and wriggle up her mini-skirt, holding me tight round the waist as I roared off, waving to the lad from Stock Control.

That Christmas, I traded in my Tiger Cub for an Ariel.

I was to see Keith just once more. He came back to the office to see us all, above all to show us his pay-slip. He had a job at Ford's in Dagenham. On a good week with bonuses, he earned as much as my monthly salary. He took us out to the car park. He had bought a Jaguar.

My story now becomes a very ordinary story: I married my typist, sold my Ariel, bought a maisonette, then a semi-detached.

But Keith, again, was a world ahead.

It was some years before I learned of it. A clichéd story, but far from ordinary.
A dark night, a souped-up car, an oily road, a placid tree ...
And me? I still have ahead of me maybe twenty years of slow, frantic pedalling.

CHACONNE IN G MINOR

ZOE LAMBERT

The End 'Chaconne in G Minor' (2015)
Gloss and masonry paint on canvas
51 x 66cm

– to the window, the yellow blind tapping against the glass. Standing there, always, leaning against the sill. Watching me, with a bloodied sun behind him. Then he takes two steps to the couch, strokes my cheek.

Tonight, he's early from work, and I'm still curled under a blanket on the couch, DVD player on pause.

You're exactly where I left you, he says.

A bad day.

So, you didn't practise?

No.

What would your mother say if she saw you like this?

He goes into the kitchen. Right, he calls. Let's cook you some dinner.

She'd say, Get up, come on, darling. Have you done your three hours? She'd say, All that money I've spent on your lessons. Do you know how much it cost? Then: Do you know if someone cut open your brain, they'd know you're a professional musician. I read that somewhere.

She'd sit on the edge of the couch, fingering the duvet, and say, Come on sweetheart, do a bit more for Mummy. And I'd say yes, of course. And then I'd lift my violin to my chin and practice my sight reading while she patted about the room, tidying the music sheets on the piano, bringing me coffee. Like she used to before the audition at Chetham's, and for the Master classes with Andras Keller. How she'd kneel in front of me before a competition, holding my hands in hers, as if in prayer. Go on, she'd say, go on. The first time I played at the

Purcell Room I searched for her in the crowd, and she gave me a little smile, saying, You can do it. Our flat a mausoleum of accomplishments. Each of my grade certificates framed along the hall. A cabinet of trophies: BBC Young Musician of the Year; Junior Winner of the Yehudi Menuhin International Violin Competition.

All the parents were like that at Chetham's. We were used to it. But on the one occasion I made a friend who wasn't a prodigious musical talent – a girl from my swimming classes in the summer holidays, she came round, eyes like big holes: *Does your mum need to put everything on the wall?*

What a handsome young man, my mother said when he came to my concert at the Royal Albert Hall. So well dressed in his suit. So smart and knowledgeable.

The first thing I said to him was, do you think you're in the Blues Brothers? He laughed at that. I'm rumbled, he said. He knows the whole film by heart. When we moved in together into this tiny flat on Princess St, I'd said surely it would bother him, my playing in the living room, and he'd said, No, I like to listen. It won't bother me at all.

And it didn't. He's a music buff. A huge CD collection. He'd had a secure job as a journalist when he was in London, but now he's moved to Manchester to be with me he pays his part of the rent by writing articles for in-flight magazines.

Have you managed to practise at all today? He calls from the kitchen. Why don't you play something for me. Some Bach, that's always uplifting.

Sure, OK.

I get up from under the blanket and pull my dressing gown around me. Still, there is that sense of hollowness, as if my insides have been dug out with a spoon. I go into the kitchen, where he is chopping an onion in hard, short slices; the tang of it stings my eyes.

I run my hands through my hair, realising it's greasy and I've not brushed my teeth today, so I go into the bathroom. I look a sight. I wash my face and rub moisturiser into it. But it doesn't make any difference; I look tired, my skin a funny yellow, jaundiced. Patches of eczema around my eyes. Lines and shadows from nights awake, lying in the dark.

Do you want some wine? I say.

He doesn't respond, so I pour two glasses. He's frying the onion now in olive oil. I drink short, sharp gulps, then pour myself another glass. Not many things as reliable as wine.

What are you making? I ask.

Bolognaise.

Can I just have pasta?

Some meat will do you good.

I swallow and look down at my hands. Such ugly hands. Knuckles like pustules from all the playing. I touch my face. My fingers are cold so I rub them together. Then I go to the corner of the room where my violin cases are leaning against the wall. I have two. One is the violin my mother bought me when I was twelve. She was working two jobs while I boarded at Chetham's. At Kendal's shoe department, then as a cleaner in the evenings. She saved and saved. She bought it off a woman who lived on our road in Irlams o'th' Height. Inside, you can read:

Ch. J.B. Collin-Mézin Luthier á Paris Rue du faubs Poissonnière, No. 10 1893

Can you imagine, my mother said. Someone playing this in the nineteenth century.

What, and dying of TB in a garret?

My mother was already ill at that point. Blood clots in her legs. At least I have you, she'd say. At least you. We were symbiotic. I played. I cared for her. She drove me to the competitions while I slept in the back of the car.

Go on, he calls. I want to hear it.

Since then, I've had a number of violins, either loaned or gifted to me. I currently have the Halle's Lincoln Strad. It sits in its case, silent and contemptuous.

As leader of the Halle, the Lincoln 1695 is for you to use, the director had said to me. I'd stood there, shaking. I immediately phoned my mother, saying, You won't believe it.

I pick up my mother's violin and position it on my shoulder. I lean my chin on the violin and try the strings. The tuner. I hear the A, and play the strings in twos till the notes fall into place.

But I can't play the Bach. All that God awful symmetry.

Music is the expression of the universe's mathematical perfection, he likes to say. A musician simply shows us this perfection.

But he's a reviewer. He spouted this kind of thing on our first date, while drinking a bottle of merlot. Beauty is symmetry and music is just showing us the beauty of maths. Bach's Goldberg Variations depend on games of symmetry to create the progression from theme to variation. Messiaen is drawn to prime numbers in Quartet of the End of Time to ...

Yeah, yeah, I said, rolling my eyes. I have a degree in music.

But he carried on anyway. I smiled, listened, drank wine till I had stains at the corners of my mouth, and he reached over to wipe them, and that was the beginning of our relationship.

I rummage through the music on the stand. And there it is.

What I want, my mother had said, is for you to play the Chaconne.

I stare at the opening bars; hearing the introductory piano chords, my internal metronome tapping away, and then my arm is attempting the opening down bow. This has to be done with gusto, power; it's a statement, and the first measure isn't tricky, not hard at all. It's a piece that builds in complexity; that performers have made even harder just to show off; but it doesn't let you rest, each measure changing, and hinting.

Why are you playing that? He calls from the kitchen. You know it gets you upset.

I stop. Then I play the next measure; the wind is ruffling the blinds; they fall back and forth on the window ledge, and behind the flats across the road, the sun is setting between the apartments.

I'm playing the Chaconne beautifully, just like she wanted.

Why are you playing this, Eloise? Why? He's placed his hand on my shoulder, his other hand holding a wooden spoon, dripping with tomato.

You're wrong, you know. It's not about the mathematical symmetry.

Let's not get into this now.

It's a journey, a story. A movement from harmony to disharmony to a new harmony. It's the relationship between consonance and dissonance. Between war and peace, and the variations in between.

By the way, your manager phoned, he says. He wants to crack on with the album before your tour starts.

He phoned you?

Well, you won't answer your phone, so yes. You're still in a contract, you know. Also, they want the Strad back.

What?

Then he comes to the kitchen door, and says, leaning against the door: You can't grieve forever.

I don't respond. I turn my back to him and swallow, and swallow again. Close my eyes against the burning, but even so, I can feel the sun through the blinds. Sometimes all I want is for there to be quiet, and for there to be still.

Sweetheart, you don't need to come, my mother had said to me that night on the phone. I'm sure it's nothing.

A stroke's not nothing.

I was sitting backstage at the Bridgewater Hall, walking around to get a good signal. I'll come after, I said. I'll be done by half nine.

Don't rush. I'm fine.

She seemed OK. She wasn't slurring her words. She was speaking and sitting up in her hospital bed, and there was the after-party. Prosecco pushed into my hand. My manager so excited at the deal; you'll be big, he'd said. So big. The next Benedetti.

We had drinks in the bar next to the Bridgewater, and then later, maybe eleven, I found missed calls on my phone.

And now, as I blink at the sheet music on the stand, I think of the things he says. *There's nothing you could have done. She wanted it that way. You can't grieve forever.*

I don't know why you keep playing that piece. Over and over, he calls from the kitchen. I just don't understand it.

I finish my second glass of wine, and say, Because grief is forever. Grief is forever, and this is why it's all bullshit. All this nonsense of albums and concerts …

But I can't explain what is wrong with this world my mother loved, that I used to love: of champagne with managers, of reviews and concerts with middle-class coughs at the ends of symphonies. What I want, the manager had said in the bar the night my mother died, is for you to pose in some part of industrial Manchester, with your violin. Black and white. Just you. Alone in the city. Looking sad and whimsical.

And what my mother said, only days before she died, is I want you to play the Chaconne in G Minor for me. It would be lovely, don't you think, at my funeral?

Of course, I said. Sure.

And I'd played it at the funeral, with a pianist accompanying me; ten minutes of time, which will loop forever in my mind.

Fine, he says, standing in front of the window. All I'm trying to do is help. Look, he says. I get you can't cope with concerts at the moment. But, you can't keep playing that piece of music over and over, destroying yourself.

Maths, I say, might underpin music.

Why are you talking about this now?

I just need to tell you …

It's like two people in different rooms, talking to you.

It's not just about the numerical relationships between notes. You think you understand music, but you don't. Maths doesn't explain grief because a mathematical equation can't tell you how pain feels.

I sink onto the couch, pull the blanket over me.

He shakes his head, slowly, as if he's tired, very tired of this conversation, and then he goes to lean against the window. The blinds shunt back and forth in the breeze, the air fluttering the slats, the lines of light falling across the room. We look at each other. I'm holding my breath inside. I think that if grief is infinite, then music is the wind behind a blind, one, two, one, two, on and on; that if music is the story of harmony being pulled apart, note by note, then rebuilt again, then the end is implicit in the beginning, and there is nothing in this hollowed out piece of wood to redeem any of that and, as I look up I see he has his back

....

(Come on, he says, why don't you play something more positive.

Irritation flares in me, so I turn and go back to the music stand to stare at the page, pain behind my eyes. This is what happens when I look too much at printed music: an immediate migraine. The doctor doesn't believe me.

From the kitchen, onions and mincemeat sizzle in the pan. The violin presses against my jaw. I can smell the comforting wood and resin, my arm poised in the air, the bow resting on the strings.)

BUT WHAT HAPPENS AFTER

JONATHAN TAYLOR

The End 'What Happens After' (2015)
Gloss and masonry paint on canvas
51 x 66cm

'But what happens after?' Ginny asked.

'What do you mean, after?' I asked. 'It's Beethoven's Fifth, for goodness sake, Ginny. There is no after. That's it. The end. Kaput, as the Germans would say.'

'Don't quote Germans at me. I've had enough of them for a lifetime. They never stop, musically or …'

'I'm not quoting. I'm just saying. That's it: perfect cadence to final C major chord, blazing triumph, the end. There's no after to Beethoven's Fifth.'

'There's the clapping we're doing now.'

'OK, but that's not part of the music.'

'And then there's us leaving here, me wheeling you out to the park, us …'

'I know, but it's not like a sequel. Music doesn't have sequels. Well, except for a few things by Wagner. The music ends, and that's it – back to life. Life and music, they're two separate things. You do talk nonsense sometimes.'

'Don't get cross with me. It's the music's fault. It's the music that makes me think like this, you know. Even when it's playing, I'm thinking it's like it's never going to end. Like Beethoven can't quite find the end, keeps looking round corners, opening doors. So the end, when it does come, feels a bit tacked on, fake, like it could actually go on forever. The tunes are still going on in my head, round and round. Do you see what I mean?'

'Not really, Ginny. Honestly, Ginny, nothing can come after an end like that. It all seems pretty final to me.'

'Nothing's ever really final,' she said.

'What do you mean?' I snapped.

'Well, look at ... I don't know ... the war, for example,' she said.

'I don't want to,' I said. 'We've come out not to look at it. It's all over now, and no one here wants to hear us talking about it. Everyone's looking at us, Ginny.'

'But it's not over,' she said, stamping her foot, as if she didn't care who was looking at us. 'Every Christmas, when it was meant to be over, it wasn't. Every bit of leave you had felt like it was over, but it wasn't. And even now all the fighting's stopped, it's not over. It'll never be over. There's no Armistice in our heads. The war, it's like a tune that keeps going round and round up there.'

'You're talking nonsense, Ginny. Getting worked up. We'll get you home. Perhaps tonight's been too much for you.'

'Don't patronise me, darling. You don't understand. You don't see that every night has been too much for me. Every night for years has been too much. And now you're back, it's still too much. I waited for you all that time, we were engaged all that time, and now you're back, it's no different. Or it is different, but it isn't.'

She cried a bit, and then grabbed her coat, pushed past a whole row of people trying to clap, and was gone.

I wasn't sure whether she was gone for good.

*

Along the line, Captain Salter is playing a gramophone record of Beethoven's Fifth back at them, across the barbed wire. He's playing it at the wrong speed, slowly-slowly-thump-thump-crackle-crackle, mocking them. When they used to play it to us before, it was like artillery fire. Now, at this r.p.m., it sounds tired, raggedy, defeated. Like them, the poor bastards.

I'm sitting – actually *sitting* – cross-legged on the top, in the hardening mud, blowing smoke rings, whistling along to the stretched-out notes, thinking that soon, so soon, the music will be over, maybe even soldiering will be over: no more tin hat, no more box respirator, I'll be demobbed and back with Ginny. She's waited a damned long time.

Before that, some of the lads have been given the job of shovelling out bits of our friends lost in the mud, dumping them into sandbags. I'll give them a hand in a sec, rolling back the wire, uprooting the posts, searching craters – and, you never know, once done, sharing a smoke with the people who were trying to kill us only a couple of days (which seems like a hundred years) ago.

None of us had believed it when the official message filtered down. No one believed the rumours of talks, church bells, flags and dancing in London, Paris. No one believed the rumours from elsewhere of white flags, collapsing lines, Mons retaken, Boche pushed back to their frontiers. Nothing like that had happened here. Here, at 11 a.m. on the 11th, it was quiet, like it used to be before the blasted planes swooped over. Further up, you could still hear muffled shelling, the machine guns, the howitzer up on the hill, all carrying on as if nothing had happened, as if they wanted to use up the ammunition while they could.

But now it really does seem to have stopped. And the guys in front of me are snipping through the wire. One of them seems to have got his leg caught. I'll go and help him in a sec.

But at this precise moment, sitting here in the sun, blowing smoke rings across No-Man's-Land, hearing Beethoven stretched on the rack to my right, I suddenly realise this is probably the happiest I will ever be.

Of course, it's all too easy to forget, mad with happiness like this, now the bloody horror is finished once and for all, that there are still mines hidden out there, waiting to blow off one's legs.

*

I couldn't chase Ginny, so I stayed where I was, whilst the clapping finished, people picked up their programmes and coats, and started to file out.

I stayed until everyone had gone, and someone was starting to brush between the rows in the gallery. He looked down at the stalls and saw me sitting there: 'Do you need any help, mate? They don't make these places for people like you.'

I shook my head, and wheeled myself out – and from there to Holland Park.

I wheeled myself to a corner of the park where Ginny and I sometimes … met. I sat facing the wall. I wanted it to block everything out.

But it didn't block everything out. I could still hear Ginny's voice.

I sat there and thought about her words, my wheels sinking into mud. It was quiet, dark. There might be a storm. Distantly, as if from across a vast no-man's-land, there came thunder. I looked up, and the gaps between the clouds above me looked like rolls of barbed wire. I looked at the wall, and the bricks were like lines of covered corpses. I looked down, and the spaces where my shins used to be were the shape of shells.

I remembered when Ginny first saw me like this in the hospital. She didn't say anything, didn't even cry. She just bent down and lightly kissed the spaces, the empty trouser legs. And, believe me or not, I felt those kisses through the skin, flesh and bone that weren't there any longer – as if the kisses were telling me that the legs weren't really gone. That nothing and no one is ever really gone.

I turned away from the wall, and headed back home.

BURNING THE ANTS
SARAH DOBBS

The End 'Burning the Ants' (2015)
Gloss and masonry paint on canvas
51 x 66cm

The girl rolls a half-empty lemonade bottle between her palms, staring at the continents of white this creates and uncreates.

Outside the café it's summer-bright. There's been a shower; the pavements lightly steam. An oil spill of foreign language, maybe Turkish. 'Ah!' a waitress says. 'I'll change it, no bother.'

It's a school day – one of the dregs left before summer – but she can't think about how to do it at home.

The swish of cars. Texts to reply to, homework, homework.

RU Coming?

Don wanna go w/out u. Lol!

Oi! Moody!

The last one hurt. Her best friend since primary who, when she told her, said: I know, it's like me, Granny Ann's in hospital. Mam was gonna keep me from school but I was like nae, I can miss the last week, woman!

Boots escalating upwards from the cellar. A thready 80s disco song tish-tishes in time with whoever's feet are pending. Joanie sips her drink, stinging her tongue with lemon, and thinks of how to kill her sister.

*

You love you love you love you love you hope you hope you hope you hope you love you love you break

*

When they were young, they wore the same clothes in 80s complementary colours. They liked Madonna's Papa Don't Preach era and Five Star but not Jackson 5. Pink and green neon, acid lemon, eye-watering brights. - *Do you like my puffball dress? - I don't like my bow, everyone will laugh.* Their ponytails, Emma's always blonder, banana-coloured, Joanie's desk-brown, so tight their hair frayed at the scalp and made them look babyish, much longer, until she started drawing on firecracker-red lipstick. Baby hair and slut-lipstick. When they were young, Emma liked milkshakes, so they would sit in high chairs, Joanie's head bent to a straw, ankles kicking the footrest, while Emma would wriggle the shoulders off her top and make boys stutter. When they were young, her sister gave Joanie Chinese burns, twisting her skin like the throttle of the bikes she'd ride that would lead to all this. She'd laugh when Joanie cried and their mother would shout up, *Be nice to your sister!* and they'd never know who she meant. Whenever Emma was uncertain, they would plait together again. But Emma was never uncertain for long. Emma flicked about, an agile koi, always moving. The one time Joanie ever really saw her sister serious, and not hatching some bold plan she would struggle to fit into, was when she was burning the ants with a magnifying glass. Joanie stepped into her light and she looked at her until she moved.

Emma is three minutes older. The hospital clock, a blank full moon, itches forward, but the hand is stuck.

*

This man smells sour, as if the healthy diet he so worships is rotting his body. He is a full-time surfer, part-time rock star. His cat, ironically, is called Sugar. His nipples are girlish-pink, like her own. She is suddenly repulsed and wants to escape, like a kitten held too long and too tight, wondering if she'll ever be set down. Before they had sex, he'd said – Do you eat meat? – I do now, she'd said. She liked the bacon barms at Sue's cafe, the brown sauce, the fat. He must imagine the meat clogging her insides, festering, gases ballooning in her arteries, the environmental impact of animal husbandry. Since Emma, she exulted in the salty pinkness of the bacon. Treasured it, like a praised child who turns a compliment over again and again. When she gets dressed, fumbling for words and clothes, she already knows they'll never speak again.

Her feet fudge the sand along the beach, there is a *shhhh* and slap of wind, sand stinging her shins.

'Naughty!' a child cries.

Her tulip skirt blossoms. She leaves it wide and old men look. She's sore. For a vegan, the man was cruel, or maybe just careless.

Two girls laugh, far away. She smiles. There's the shush of the sea. The sea. She passes a family, the conversation becoming bold then faint.

'No, love, he'll be sick.'

'U-huh.'

'So like, a was thinking. We'll have the dragon on one side, the other –'

'The beach?'

'The *beach*.'

'U-huh. And then ...'

She feels a pinch of hate for this girl. This girl is understood, she is loved.

The backwards crunk as shutters on beachside businesses are heaved up.

A sign in a just-opening amusement arcade: *Balls gone soft? Try ours. In stock now!*

A little heartbeat of music somewhere. She listens; Morrisey's mournfulness – and shuts it out.

An American accent saying, 'yoghurt.'

A man nods. 'Aye pet, you've made ma day.'

She draws her skirt over the soreness between her legs. A plastic bag kites in the sky above her head. She looks at the lighthouse with its red cap. Irises brighten nearby benches, tied like hostages to the scroll arm.

*

'Emma? Emma?'

Their mother nods. 'She can hear you.'

'Em? S'me.'

'D'you want some time alone?'

'Yeah,' she lies.

It was everything they'd ached for, Emma opening her eyes. You have a very small window with which to emerge from a coma, so the doctors had said. Of course Emma had made it. But they hadn't expected this, waiting on the other side of that. Her sister lies, still as the clock, blinking, her breath getting wetter-sounding. Her eyes, the only parts of her body that can still move, swivel left to right in her head like a comedy robot.

*

Joanie goes somewhere else every day. Today she's bussed it to another beach; two weeks of summer holidays already eaten into.

She points towards the sea and marches, hunched against the wind. A little clatter of plate against plate in a back room from one of the cafe huts. Girls' laughter. The wind drops. A cyclist zips by, back a tense bridge shape, faster than the sports car cruising the marina.

When she pulls her hair from her eyes and mouth, seeking out the laughter, they've gone. She buys a candyfloss-flavoured ice cream that tastes of vanilla and feels plasticky on her tongue.

She is nearly back at the stop when she sees a boy, maybe seventeen, just a bit older than her. He's French-brown, as if European. Shorts and vest despite the lengthening fret, towing a fat brown lab. It's only after a few moments she notices the cane, the queer wobble to his head. Why do our bodies do these things to us? She wishes she could know him, how he talks and what he talks about. The cold deepens; the first spits of rain. She opens up her palms and lets it patter patter onto her.

Signs run along the length of Marine View – VISIT St Peter's Cathedral, VISIT Winter Gardens, VISIT Herrington Country Park.

She opens up her notebook, writes:

Visit: St Peter's cathedral.

Visit: Winter Gardens

Visit: Herrington Country Park.

*

Emma always was the stubborn one.

'Hi, sis.'

Emma does not reply. She can. They have a thing now, which connects to her eye movements. If she wanted, she could look out 'Hi' back; it'd only take about half an hour and a well-spoken voice that wasn't her sisters would say 'Hi.' Joanie's been on forums about it. You can get fancy ones with other people's voices. It just takes time. Emma looks at the little Siamese fighters she'd brought in for her. Watching their bodies twist and flick and propel and soar in water. She didn't think she'd done it to be cruel. The reality, if she was honest, that she hadn't thought about it at all.

It was mum's day off from the hospital. She had killed guilty time, nails drumming as though checking each fingertip for sensation, in the canteen, where time did not count in the same way as it did outside the automatic doors and the haze of cigarettes. She half-watched a family – matriarchal, making-the-best-of, spooning hospital ice cream sundaes.

She had texted boys back:
Sure.
Maybe.
Nae Botha.

Like the girls on the beach, when she'd looked again, there'd just been empty sundae glasses, an impression of what was once there. She'd balled her serviette and tossed it, walking on automatic to the lifts, pressing call, deciding she should walk, it was rude not to. The trudge of each stair.

'Em?'

Her sister's eyelashes fan open and closed, open and closed. Her tear ducts are faulty now; she can't even cry. They have to put in drops. They have to guess when, because she won't use the machine unless the doctors are in to make her.

'Going home soon, aren't you Emma? That'll be nice, all your own things.' The nurse says. She the one with the green-blue eyes that their father has commented upon, like the friend from Byker they'd made when they were in Mallorca. Her eyes so unusual Joanie wonders if it's her. What'd her name been? Gemma? She wonders, did the universe do these things to you, bring people back together without them even knowing?

She cannot sit, cannot just be. Her, who would loll and read and nap and snack, cannot now live with traffic jams. She'd ding the bell and get off the bus. No queues either - *I'll leave it thanks*. Or - *I'll be back*, never to return. There is a boot camp sergeant major straight as an exclamation mark making a fist in her head. Move move move!

'I'll be back.' A kiss to Emma's forehead. Wake up, sleeping beauty, except this one's already awake.

She propels round a Tesco, seizes things that are Lycra, strips in the supermarket toilets that have a smear of blood on the sanitary towel bin. In the air, in the world, she pulls off her sandals and runs barefoot to the lighthouse until her lungs scream and she's forced to keel over, choking with emotion.

Dry-puking onto silver and carmine – fish guts. It is the most alive she's ever been. Fisherman's lines zing, catch and release. She wonders how it must feel to have a hook slice your cheek, whether one of their lines ever catch a someone, not a fish.

Walking in a random direction, down someone's street, she notices a Suzuki motorbike, black and yellow, chained up at the free parking bays. Emma, how you can ride tha thing when you know what it puts me through? Wait until you're a mam. No motherhood now, mam, though Emma had never been traditional.

Joanie peers at the bike, circles it, till a man peers out at a nearby kitchen window. She waves like they're best friends. He puts up a hand: stop.

*

'Woooo!' When the bike pulled off, it left her stomach in the same place. His name is Eric, and she dipped with his knee bends, left and right, left and right. The coast road licked out, a flashing adder's tongue. Slowing, she caught hold of the back seat, her stomach caught up too.

A dog is barking, there is a woman peering through the sand dunes, in need of a wee, she imagines. The leather creaks. A lace of salt in the air. A man brings a baby back towards a jeep.

She shucks off the helmet, unclips a strand of hair from her lip, leaves the rest a mess.

'Could walk the beach?' he says.

She watches a man take a picture of a young boy, maybe his grandson, frothing up the sand dunes. St Aidan's the sign says near the paths. *Open to the public.*

She wants to ask, will you take my picture? 'We could,' she says, and sand steeps over her toes. They strip out of their leathers, carry them under one arm. When they crest the dunes there is a whole world of water, it seems. Maybe the same dog, a spaniel, that was barking before flaps after two small birds.

Two tiny birds, their tiny hearts in their tiny feathered chests exploding with shock as their wings nip them up and right and away. The dog's ears flip-flop like lazy rabbits. A couple join up with the spaniel; they hold another on its lead. The spaniel circles back.

'Bit more sheltered in here,' Eric says.

It is sunny but cold. There are goosebumps on her legs. She wants to look out to Holy Island and think of Emma, give her the view she has now. But she is cold and he is warm. She wants to feel her cold skin against his hot stomach.

There is a twizzling sound from birds, clogged conversation from a passing family, the *tap tap pant pant* of paws and dog, a sharp whistle and it arcs away. A small piece of her, kissing and kissing to ease the hunger, goes with it. What do you see dog, what can you see?

*

When they were young, Emma would spin Joanie round and round on the dunes, eyes bound to smear black. Every now and then a star of sunshine beat through the cracks. Black, bright, black. Her feet unsteady, heels jamming sand and grass. Most of the time, she spilled dead level where she'd started. Once, she careened over the edge like a runaway barrel, arms and legs starfishing out. She finally stopped on the flat beach, feet out, woozy, huffing hard. Never loved her sister more than then.

*

Their mother has a rack of anti-ageing creams, like some people have herbs and spices. Q-something, retinol this, + that. She imagines the creams, sitting on top of their mother's skin, filling in the age. Temporary, like how buttercream melts when you lick it. For some reason, these creams are now lined up in the dining room that is to become Emma's.

Joanie is the shadow in the house, leaning against the doorframe watching half of their mother – only half is visible as she bends and twists – as if doing something every-day like exercising, stretching out her calf muscles. Aaaand the other leg. There is a rustle as games they'd long grown out of, paperwork, napkin rings, go into a big bag.

'Make yourself useful,' their mother says, but Joanie has dissolved.

In the treehouse their father built in the garden, where Emma brought boys and Joanie watched the shifting light and shadow. Now, she waits, chin on their bedroom window-ledge, she waits for her sister's homecoming, wondering when she would catch up. Now, she's still waiting, soothing cream over wrinkles yet to exist, but feeling the shapes of Emma's face under her fingertips. She had never needed a mirror before, but Emma's face was slack, changed.

*

She is brought in as though she's already dead, straight, delivered on a nice trolley. Sign here, please. Their father has apparently very important work up in Dundee. He has a lot of work in Dundee lately. They're opening a new branch, their mother says when they sometimes meet in the kitchen. Her fat cheeks are pitting. When the man has gone and Emma is all plugged in, Joanie follows her mother into the kitchen. She's making a whole worktop of tuna mayonnaise sandwiches *just-in-case*. Cut into triangles, their shapes echoed with kitchen towels folded over the same.

She wants to hug their paling mother, thin as a watercolour painting. If she does, she knows instinctively that their mother will either break, or that she will stand, straight until she lets go. Just bones and duty.

'Can I have one?'

'Go and keep your sister company.'

'You know mum, we don't have to sit in there with her the whole time. She needs to sleep.'

'And so what? I'm not looking after her? I'm the one up all night while everyone else sleeps.'

'I know, I just. Just ... maybe your snoring keeps her awake?'

'Don't you think I know that?' Their mother poked her chest with the butter knife.

*

At night, Joanie lies awake in her single bed. Emma is directly below. There will be the hiss and shift of the air bed, a formula of LEDs that let them know she is alive without staring at her chest, the light of the small TV and their mother's soaps, seeping from one working class nightmare to the next. She can hear their mother snoring – great, cracking rips – from Emma's new room. In the morning, she'll deny she slept at all.

At two, there is a car sound, brakes, light, the garage. The front door going then going again. Their parents will sit and smoke in the front.

She slips down. She sits in her mother's cooling seat.

The electronic voice that is now Emma's says, 'Her fuc-king snor-ing.'

And Joanie laughs till her nose stings. She takes her sister's fingers, which are cold. I run hot, Emma would say, hands proud on hips, half joking, always 'just off out', with a backwards wink. Joanie was the girl with the water bottles and whiny pleas to turn up the heating, secretly wishing Emma would have her heart broken by one of the boyfriends and come back to her.

'I – am – still - here,' the machine says.

I miss you, Joanie had been thinking.

'Tell – me – a-bout – life.'

'My life?'

'Yes – stu-pid.'

Joanie listens, the soft blur of her parents chatting, the blue of smoke rising to the crescent of glass at the front door, the stitch of a shoe scraping gravel. Their father would be stood up, flicking ash into the lavender.

'I met this – man.'

*

'Ya not like other girls,' he nods at her, sucking a roll-up and squinting just as much, as if it's a spliff. They're standing up high by the bike in its stand, a Ninja, she's learned, blue-slanted menace. They're a still from a film. He looks like James Dean if he hadn't died, down to the brill-creamed blonde quiff. Stubble glitters like sand. Stupid as fuck but proper soft, like. Seaham at sunset, overlooking crashing surf, which spits so high against the lighthouse she wonders if there's an oversized whale blowing upwards, choosing just that moment to breathe. They're just before the Tommy statue by Ridgeley, bought by the town because they couldn't bear to let it go. A soldier with such age and weariness lining his face, it makes her think of these people, the locals she never quite fit in with. The strength of these old pit towns though, where beauty grows between the cracks. They have been to the Winter gallery and creaked around in leather at the pink pottery this place is known for. She wonders if he can read so well, his texts are like her – young: *lol, u gud hen? x*

'So a –' Suck and blow. 'A seen you like, what, three times now?' He flicks ash with his thumb. 'You gan tell me your name anytime soon?'

What he wants to say, she thinks, is, we fucked, why won't you tell me your name? Why don't *you* want me?

'But it's kinda cool, aye.'

She hates him for a split second, the way you're repulsed by someone else drinking out of your bottle and then handing it back to you, slippy. You want to at least wipe the spit away, but people are watching, so you drink, their germs invading yours.

She lifts her chin, the plucky heroine. 'You wanna know my name?'

He regards her, twisting out the roll-up under his boots. The smoke obscures his face and she imagines it clinging to, darkening, his hair.

'Emma.'

'Emma.' He nods at his fingers in the roll-up tin, teasing up tobacco like plucking a nipple. 'Suits ya.'

When they fucked, sometimes she held onto him like he was someone else. Someone she hadn't yet met, whose forehead she longed to press kisses against, whose soul had knitted into her bones like a cancer. The books in the library said love was like that, but she didn't know. Maybe Emma did. Maybe she'd ask.

Later, they sped, zipping up the places they'd been, creating a new road. Only forwards. Stopping, kissing. She holds onto him when he's inside her, cups his jaw, thumbs away the creases this makes in his blonde brows. 'Love you,' he breathes against her neck, breath foggy-black with cigarettes.

'My sister's the plain one,' she says, when they dress, hopping up into jeans, grinning at each other fastening buttons, him unthreading grass from her hair.

'What's her name?'

'Doesn't matter.'

He laughs.

'It *doesn't*!' She blushes.

'Who's got your knickers in a twist – apart from me?'

She folds her arms. 'Why don't we ever go back to yours? Why's it always on the bloody beach?' She shakes her head and pushes past him to grab one boot, the other.

The camera would pan out, a panorama, the blue majestic given over to sudden leaden skies, maybe a close-up of barbed wire surrounding the industrial estate across from the farm, where they'd propped the bike.

'A care for me mam, she's a handful at best of times like.'

Her back to him. 'I like the way you say "mam".'

'Everyone says "mam". Mam. Gan. What da you say?'

She could tell him about Emma now; it was the right time. Truth for truth. How she'd hoped since forever to be the most important, the only one, to matter, to come first. How this could all be her fault. He'd understand and it would be okay. But then, apart from these occasional moments were it felt good – special – to be the one her parents got to keep, there was that awful yawn of responsibility. How could she ever make up for Emma?

'Let's go for a swim at Hendon.'

'Nae, you can swim there. Them currents. There's nae lifeguard.'

'Who'll know?'

True dare double dare.

Her stomach pinches. She can't remember the last time she ate. She drinks milk through straws, sips soup. She can't stand to sit down for a meal.

In Hendon, hunger forgotten, she blasts into water, submerged so it fills her ears and darkens her hair, the shock of it, the salt of it, the space where things slow down. She manages to open her eyes, sees a shape through the murk. Two arms, praying towards her. Or Eric doing breaststroke. She basks in the hum of gloopy quiet, the slow drum of her heart, the languorous beat of dulled sound.

The world explodes. 'Jesus, ye got a death wish?'

She pants for breath, thinking how nobody could ever understand how alive she feels right now. For just a second, she'd imagined his shape to be Emma's, crabbing towards her.

*

The clock loses its reign in summer, she swam and rode and bemused Eric and got to like his old face and his boy bravado when really he was just a man living at home with his mam, tethered. A rockstar on a bike. At nights, at some time, were the conversations with her sister.

'Where – do – you – exist – anyway?'

Joanie is on the airbed, the two of them paired like socks, like they would on Christmas day before it was OK to wake mum and dad. She is looking at Emma's so-pretty face, ruined by blankness. What had made her beautiful, irresistible, Joanie thinks, always the plainer, was her actions. A cartoonist would draw two lines behind her to indicate speed. A jutting chin. It was as if she knew.

'I always existed in my head.' Joanie is sleepy and Eric combs into her thoughts, washes out again, while she waits.

'I – in – body. Now – in – brain.'

'Is it enough?'

The toilet flushes.

'I've been looking it all up, Em. I read that it takes people a while, like a year to adjust. We can wait – we can just see.'

They don't have long. Their mother has roused from one of her non-naps, *only closed my eyes*, as if sleeping is desertion of love. Their father is god-knows-where again, *you know your father*. Did they? Was he sitting in a layby somewhere sobbing that he wasn't man enough to fix his daughter's pain? Why had this happened to them? What had he done? What could he do?

*

Her sister has tiny blonde hairs at her wrists, the wrists are feminine, you could wrap your thumb and forefinger about them with an overlap. She has a twin-freckle on her earlobe, see, your sister knew, their mam would say. She has clear, small pores, except around her nose where there are peppered blackheads. Her lips get dry and the skin flakes. Joanie has worked on Vaseline and pulled at them, guilty when this draws blood. Emma's teeth smell; they have forgotten to brush them. She is decaying but preserved.

*

When they were young Emma set fire to ants with a magnifying glass and Joanie had watched. She attracted the ants with a half-finished strawberry split. Lick lick, lick, nibble. A long final lick, with relish. She placed it on the ground and assembled herself, cross-legged. – Pass me that paper. Joanie retrieved The Herald from the front step and Emma tore away little strips. She produced the magnifying glass and checked the sky. Joanie had laughed when there was smoke. – You're in my light, and she'd flinched away, unable to turn, despite saying – that's gross, I'm telling. In bed that night, it was the only time Joanie had ever seen Emma sister cry. She hung over the bunk bed; Emma liked the bottom.

'What?' Emma unrolled to look up, hands captured under one ear.

'I'm sad about the ants.'

'So why'd you do it?'

'I thought you should know what it's like.'

'I need a wee. What what's like?'

'To kill something.' And her eyes blink-blinking, dark and big.

*

The days slip into weeks and the sky goes from hot-blue to bland, like someone has twisted the dial of their grandparents' old TV between stations. She starts college. Their mother has bought her new jeans that rise up a little too high on the ankles. On her first day, their mother twisted in her chair, and brushed a goodbye her way.

Joanie climbs the high steps at college every day and looks out onto the town, missing the sea and how it can toss her body, tug at her legs, how she has to fight it. She looks at everybody with their lives, the playful fighting between girls and lads she's noticed in some of her classes. Someone asks a casual question, a boy with a happy face and floppy hair – *Got'nee brothers a sisters?*

She starts sitting with a girl called Penelope, because she talks without spaces to fill, about tests and exams and futures and other people's poor cosmetic choices. People start to wear scarves. Eric has bought her a wetsuit, boots, a hood. She won't wear it because he's bought it. *Freeze a fuckin nips off she will*, he says, as though she's not even there.

Emma is just the same, only the skin is somehow thinning, moulding itself onto the bones beneath. She has such lovely bone structure, her mother says, stroking Emma's brow with a cloth.

'I won't wear the wetsuit,' she whispers to Emma. 'I'm saving up for my own.' 'Good. You – don't – need – him. Always – more – in-de-pen-dent – than me.'

For some reason, this makes Joanie glow like a candle. Something beaming in their darkened house. You made me this way, she thinks, fashioned out of love and steel.

'But – fuck it. Take – the – gift.'

She laughs, briefly so happy, she wants to cry.

'I – have – dec-i-ded – Joa-nie.'

'It's not been long, Em. Remember we said it could take a while to get used to things?'

'Used – to – this?'

They have never said it outright. But she knows, they know.

The next bright day, she buys a Cornetto from the shop and curls some of the cream onto her tongue. She peers into the chalky sky and waits for the travelling sun, the appearing ants. Would there even be any in winter? Her eyes are glassy. She lowers the magnifying glass. They'd all be buried safe in the ground till spring.

'What're you doing?' Their mother's voice is brittle.

She stills and their mother goes back inside.

'Trying to practice,' she says.

*

It is spring again. The girl is in the surf, fighting current, water spilling, rippling all around her body, she dinks below the waves and the underwater roars – life roars – in her chest, her ears, her brain. She kicks out, diving deeper, rolling over, darting like a flashing fish. Breath all stopped up until she crests the surface and it fizzes. She's gasping and laughing, brushing water from her face.

HARBOUR LIGHTS
AJ ASHWORTH

The End 'Harbour Lights' (2015)
Gloss and masonry paint on canvas
51 x 66cm

THE END: FIFTEEN ENDINGS TO FIFTEEN PAINTINGS

Some nights Didier dreams he is at Harbour Lights again. Moving through the sea of tables and chairs as fluidly as an eel, teeming plates of golden fish and chips in his hands, some balanced on his forearms like one of the circus performers he might have seen as a small boy on a day trip into Paris with his father. His father is long dead now. He struggles to recall his face sometimes, on those evenings when he thinks of him – when the light is low, when there is no television. When he is not thinking of the woman for the briefest time; the woman who brought him here to the grey Yorkshire coast, who steered him away from France and his father, the woman who has now also, somehow, steered herself away from him.

And always in these dreams of his, there is that feeling – that small rise and swell of fear – that one of the plates will unbalance and tip away from him towards the floor. The crockery smashing against the white tiling, the batter breaking open until the pale flesh of the haddock spills out. And the thought comes to him then that he will reach to save the falling plate but in doing so will lose all the others he holds. But there is only ever the threat of ruin; no plate ever falls to the floor. Even so, the dreams trouble him. And Didier wakes afterwards with damp in his palms and over his forehead. The arm that held the trembling plate trapped beneath the bulk of his belly, half-dead and tingling from the weight of him. He always turns onto his back then and massages it until the feeling returns, in the way she would have done if she were there. Pushing her fingertips into his skin, kneading and pressing, then perhaps kissing the crook of his elbow when it was all right again, when the blood was flowing into it once more.

It has been two months since he stopped working at the restaurant. Two months of sitting in the living room. Two months of forcing himself out to walk the town while avoiding the pier that he would often walk with her; sometimes returning to sit in her car to inhale the salt smell of her, turning over the engine from time to time but never able to make himself drive it. Two months of low appetite and broken sleep. Sometimes, he makes himself a hot chocolate for breakfast, in the hopes it will waken his taste buds but it doesn't and he can only manage a few sips before pouring the chocolate away down the sink; the dark brown pooling around the plughole before draining away.

'Tartare sauce? Ketchup? Bread and butter?' Sometimes he catches himself saying the words out loud. The words he always said to diners as he delivered their plates of steaming food. Sometimes they would say no or yes to one or all. And he would bring the bread or the sauces before eventually leaving them with their cod or their haddock or their sole, saying to them, 'Enjoy your dinner', never 'Bon appétit', even though some of them might have expected him to, if they had noticed his accent or thought, as she did, that he looked just like a typical Frenchman.

'You just need a beret and a string of onions,' she'd laughed early on, teasing him for his combed black hair and moustache, his dark Gallic eyes. 'If I buy you a stripy top will you wear it?'

'No,' he'd said and pulled her to the bed, a hand to her hip. 'Absolument pas.' But, still, she had bought him one – blue lines on it the colour of the English Channel – and, yes, he had worn it for her in the way he never would have for anyone else. And now, all these years later, he wears it for her still.

'Tu es sûr?' his father had asked Didier on the morning almost twenty years ago now when he was to leave for England, for the woman waiting for him there. 'Are you sure this is what you want?'

Didier had gripped the handle of the small case resting in his lap and turned to his father, trying not to see the deep lines at the sides of his mouth, the mass of grey bristles over his face and neck. 'Yes,' he said. 'I am.'

His father had nodded, not taking his eyes from the backs of his hands on the steering wheel. 'You hardly know her ... but it's your life and you're old enough I suppose ... you're not a child. Not anymore.'

Didier had shook his head a little. 'No,' he'd said, thinking of the woman again – how she had looked that first time he saw her, at the farm door just a few weeks before: the shorts, the muddied boots, the backpack dropped at her feet; the velvet sound of her voice as she asked for milk and a place to sleep for the night, her grey eyes on his as she reached for the right words and the right way to say them to him.

Didier had tried not to stare at her, tried to breathe the heat out of his face. Then, when he showed her in and poured a glass of milk, he tried not to let her see how his hand shook. But it was pointless to try and hide anything from her. Those grey eyes saw everything. He could tell from the way she smiled as she took the glass of milk and drank it without looking away from him. And he could tell again days later as he moved over her in the spare room, when she held him and touched his cheek after, when he knew that she had seen into him and realised that she had been his first. Those eyes of hers didn't miss a thing.

'I'll come and visit,' Didier said to his father before climbing out of the pickup to go and get his boat. 'And you can always come to England and ...' He half moved his hand towards him but was unable to make it go any further. The sad lump at his father's throat stopped him from doing or saying anything more.

His father nodded, glanced at him briefly then reached for the key in the ignition.

'Goodbye, Father.'

But his father did not take his eyes from the windscreen. 'I hope you'll be happy there.'

And Didier nodded before getting out and walking towards his ferry, turning back to wave at him before he went inside. But his father was no longer there: his pickup was already shrinking on its journey back to the farm and away from him.

It was nine months later when Didier and the woman were woken during the night by a phone call from one of the neighbouring farms. The man – Fabrice – telling him how his father had managed to drive to him before his heart had closed finally like a fist. Didier listened without saying anything then hung up, the woman holding onto him as if to stop him from falling to the floor. It was days before he was able to speak, months before he was able to accept that he would never see his father alive again.

The two of them had tried for a child. It was what they wanted and it seemed the right thing after such a loss as that. Girl or boy, they would name it for Didier's father: Jean or Jeanne. It would have her features and Didier's colouring, it would be taught to speak both languages from infancy. And it would have a happy life – that was certain. The child would be more loved than it was possible to be and by parents who themselves loved each other.

They would joke about this child that would one day sigh and roll its eyes at them, that would tut when they were too caring or protective. But it was clear to them: they would love it with full and open hearts and it would come before anything and everything else in their lives. The child would be blessed to have them and they would be blessed to have it. Fatherhood – never even a consideration for Didier while he was with his father on the farm – was here now, bright and promising as a moon. Brought to him by this woman who had backpacked around his country until she walked up the lane towards his farm and found him.

If someone opened him up and looked inside him he was sure they would see fireworks and sparklers there instead of lungs and a heart. That was how being with the woman made him feel, that was what the thought of having a child with her did to him.

Each month, though, the blood would come. And the woman would go into the bathroom after feeling the small, wet bloom of it arrive in her underwear. Emerging afterwards with just a smile or a shrug after the first few times, resignation and paleness when the months turned to years. The small, white sticks she had bought remained in their packets in the bathroom cabinet. But after five years of trying, Didier watched from the doorway as she took them out one by one and dropped them into a binbag; touching her on her arm as she passed him on her way to take the bag out to the bin in the yard. The talk of children at an end. Never to be mentioned again.

They never found out what their own particular reasons for childlessness were. Didier offered to go for tests while they were still trying and once even suggested that she might want to try and find another man instead – one who could give her what she wanted. But she had taken both of his hands in hers and kissed the backs of them, her grey eyes wide when she looked up at him once more. 'No,' she'd said. 'There is no other man.' And heat had flooded his eyes and chest as he nodded at her, a light trembling at his lip. And he knew then that he would never need to imagine a time when the woman would not be there with him, when she would not want to be in his life.

It was ten years into their time together that Didier woke in the night to the sound of the woman breathing raggedly beside him in sleep, as if sobbing. He touched her and she quietened before turning onto her back, her breath slowing and deepening once more. In the morning, he asked her what she had been dreaming about but she said she didn't know at first. 'I do remember a fishing boat though,' she added, holding the mug of tea to her chest as if trying to warm herself with it. 'It was night and it was coming into harbour, but all its lights were out – and the harbour lights too. I was on the pier ... I could only just make it out. But its engine,' she said, clenching her jaw. 'I remember now ... its engine was so loud that it frightened me. I thought my ears were going to burst.' She stared over towards the window but there was a glassiness in her eyes as if she wasn't seeing it at all. 'I thought it was going to come straight at me and crash into the pier. I remember thinking I just wanted a light to come on somewhere so I could see ... but there was nothing but dark and the sound of that engine. I hope I never hear a sound like that again.'

The woman had to lie inside a machine when she found the first lump, a few weeks after the dream. Didier held her hand before she went in, told her that everything was going to be all right. He hoped that saying it would make it true. But when he saw her afterwards, there were dark dips beneath her eyes, a pallid look to her skin. She no longer seemed to be the woman she always had been, as if something had become lost inside her.

'In there,' she said, unable to finish her sentence. It was the first thing she had been able to say to him.

'Dis-moi.' He squeezed her hand but she did not squeeze back.

'It ...' She swallowed. 'It sounded like that boat.'

'Boat?' he'd asked, not sure what she meant. He thought of the boats that slipped in and out of the harbour almost every day of the year but nothing would come.

'The one in my dream.'

He remembered what she had told him about the dream then – the low rumble of the boat, the lack of light. He told her again that she was going to be fine, that there was nothing to worry about but it was almost as if she wasn't able to hear him.

'Being in there was like being in the dark again on that pier.'

'They're going to help you, mon chou,' he said, cupping one of her hands with both of his. 'They're going to make you better.'

'It's like that banging's inside me now, that sound,' she said. She was staring towards a curtained window. 'It's like I'll never be able to get rid of it.'

Didier kissed the narrow valley that ran below her ear, between jaw and neck. He nuzzled his nose softly into it as if he was some kind of gentle animal. 'It's just a sound,' he said. 'Everything's going to be alright.'

She stroked the side of his face, slowly – her touch as cool as raindrops. 'I've always had a feeling something would happen, something out of the blue ... at least now I know what that something is.'

Didier wakes now after another of the dreams at Harbour Lights. His hard, round belly heavy on his arm; his hand tingling once more. This time the woman was in the dream too – sitting at one of the tables: her back to him, hair tied in a bun, small wisps of curls resting against her neck. He tried to walk in her direction but before he could, one of the plates he was holding trembled and started to tip away from him; the fish and chips slipping on the porcelain until a light streak of grease trailed out from behind them. As he leaned to try and steady the plate, the others began to tremble too and it was as all of them began to tilt and fall away from him – in a way they never had before – that the woman moved her head in his direction. Didier's eyes opened though before she could see him, before he had chance to feel those grey eyes of hers on him one more time.

He wipes his forehead and glances at the clock: 22:01. He has only slept for fifteen minutes or so but is fully awake now. He knows there will be no more sleep for him tonight, not now that he has dreamed the woman back into his life again. He stands and goes to the window, lifts the curtain a little and glances out. There is a crescent moon hanging low in the sky, thin as a fingernail. He remembers the sight of the woman's hands, how they would look as they rested in his, how the tips of her own fingernails were as thin and white as that moon is now. He lets the curtain fall and starts to get dressed. He needs to go outside, needs to try and rid himself of the dream, the sensation of pressure that is there on his chest now, as if something heavy and winged has flown in and alighted there.

He leaves and steps out into the car park. He is halted by the sight of the woman's white car in their bay where she left it the last time she drove it, months ago now, to her last appointment. For a long time he has avoided looking at it, avoided trying to think about what to do with it. But there is something about the way the faint moonlight touches it now that makes him realise he will not be able to ignore it anymore. It looks otherworldly in this light, ghostly almost – as if it is not quite of this world or any other. If he touches it now, he is sure his hand will go through it as if through mist. That is how strange it looks in the night, how pale.

He takes his keys out and moves towards it. He places the key in the lock and opens the door, his heart thumping as he gets inside and reaches for the ignition. It will not start this time, he is sure of it. But he turns the key and the engine rumbles into life. His hand trembling as he takes the handbrake off and lets the car roll back out of the space. The brakes grinding, the creak of metal, but there is life in this car yet. It has not seized up as he thought it might have done after having been neglected for so long.

He pulls out of the car park then and drives through the dark streets of the town. He can see the blue blink of televisions through thin curtains, the warm glow of overhead lights and table lamps. He continues and before long realises he is driving towards the harbour and the small row of parking spaces huddled together not far from Harbour Lights and the pier. He pulls in and sits there for a time, the small orange lights on the dashboard greying out as he turns the key to off. He gets out and locks the door, lets his eyes wander towards the first few weather-beaten planks of the pier – from where he and the woman would often start to watch for the comings and goings of boats.

'Didier!' a voice comes from behind him then. He turns. It is Derek, the owner of Harbour Lights – his jacket over his arm and car keys in his hand as he moves in Didier's direction. It must be ten-thirty – the usual time Derek leaves the restaurant when it has been a good night, when takings have been high and nothing untoward has happened in the kitchen.

'Ah, hello,' says Didier.

'How are you?' There is a warmth in Derek's voice and face that makes Didier's throat tighten a little.

'I'm fine ... well, you know ... yes, I'm alright.'

Derek squeezes the top of Didier's arm for a moment before letting go. 'We miss you,' he says, small sparkles of light in his eyes. 'You know you're welcome back any time ... any time at all. If you ever want to that is.'

Didier nods and smoothes his fingers down his moustache. 'Yes,' he says. 'Thank you ...'

'What have you been up to? Are you managing to get out? I haven't seen you for a long time ...' He glances down towards Didier's shoes. Didier follows his gaze and sees what his old friend will also have seen, even in the dimness: that his left shoe is blue, the other black.

'Oh, I've just ... you know ... not been doing much,' says Didier, heat seeping into his face. But when he looks up again, Derek's eyes are no longer on his shoes but are passing over the car instead.

'Is that Maura's? I thought you might have ...' But he doesn't finish his sentence.

Didier manages a nod. 'Yes ... I thought I'd just take it for a drive ...'

Derek continues looking at the car, his lips pressed tight together. His Adam's apple dips and he opens then closes his mouth as if unsure how to say something. 'It was cruel what happened,' he says finally. 'The way it took her like that. To think she was in the clear for so long and then ... cruel.' He shakes his head.

Didier glances towards the pier. 'Yes,' he says, unable to say anything more.

'You loved her ... she loved you – that much was obvious to anyone ... we should all be so lucky to have something like that.'

A cloud the colour of ashes passes over the moon. Didier watches as it lengthens and thins before dispersing altogether.

'Don't let it ruin your life as well, Didier,' says Derek. 'Please ... one life is enough ...'

Derek puts his hand on Didier's shoulder before nodding, getting into his car and driving away towards his home on the edge of town.

Didier rests his hand against the cool edge of the car's roof, unsure what to do now – to get back in and go home again or to leave the car there and walk. A sound off in the dark of the water makes him lift up and walk towards it. It is a low sound yet, like a distant aeroplane. But it grows a little louder the further he walks and soon he is at the start of the pier, his stomach listing as he contemplates putting a foot onto it. It is like stepping out into an abyss, making that step onto the first plank after so long of not doing. The last time he walked it was with the woman. But he is on it now and moving forward, following that sound like a fish nosing through water. And before long he is up near the end of the pier, the water black and churning beyond it, the rumbling sound increasing although he cannot yet see where it is coming from.

He puts his hands onto the icy rail and peers into the night – the moon has slipped out of sight so not even the small amount of light from its crescent will help him to see now. The sound grows louder, reaching above the white noise hiss of the water. He moves his eyes in the direction he thinks it is coming from and can see something pale and moving in the air above the water now. He tightens his grip on the rail, a cold trickling down the back of his neck. It is like a small patch of glowing mist that is growing in size the nearer it comes. 'Maura,' the thought comes from somewhere. 'She is coming for me.' Even though he knows the mist is not the woman at all; still the sight of it makes goosebumps rise in a small, cold wave down the length of his spine.

The patch grows larger and the sound associated with it vibrates inside his body now. Whatever the light is, it is getting nearer. He thinks of returning to the car, of going home, but he cannot seem to take his hand from the rail. He carries on watching. There is a shape beneath the patch of light now; separating itself out from the blackness of the water. He tightens his hold on the rail and the shape draws nearer. An engine – that is what the sound is. And the shape, a boat: a late one coming in with its haul of plaice and haddock, its brown crab and scallops. Didier stares into the moving patch of mist above it and the shape becomes clearer: it is the pale bodies of gulls lit from below by the lights of the boat; the birds circling above it in the hope that they will be thrown something from the day's catch.

Didier takes his hand from the rail and breathes out. His lungs ache as if he has been holding his breath. The boat passes him on its way into the harbour. There are fishermen in orange waterproofs in the back of it, bending over as they sort through the slick mounds of fish and crustaceans. One of the younger ones is humming a tune that Didier doesn't recognise. A slow, mournful tune that makes him think of the woman, of the feel of her hand in his, the taste of her skin on his lips. Didier begins walking back down the pier, glancing in the direction of the woman's car as he does so but it no longer has the eerie look to it that it had before, not now that the moon has disappeared out of sight.

He hears a shout then from the boat and sees the younger fisherman standing now and lifting something up towards the gulls before throwing it at them. The fisherman stands there with his mouth open as a bird breaks away from the swirling group of them and dives for the food. It catches the piece of fish and is gone, away from the boat and into the shadows. The young fisherman laughs loud and long, claps his hands for a moment before bending and beginning to sort through the catch once more, starting up with his slow, sad humming again.

Didier is almost at the start of the pier now. A few more steps and he will be off the wooden planks and back on concrete. More steps still and he will be at the door of the woman's car and opening it up, driving away. He looks over towards the boat again, the boat that is beginning to slow and turn now as it pulls in for home. He can still see the young fisherman in the back, his eyes bright as he hums that unknown song while the night spins slow and certain above him. The young fisherman's hands move through the gleaming bodies of the fish that lie on the deck of the boat below him, slowly, carefully, in the same way they will on all the trips that are yet to come. Just as those hands that follow him will. On these same dark waters, under these same dark skies.

DECOMPRESSION CHAMBER

ASHLEY STOKES

The End 'Decompression Chamber' (2015)
Gloss and masonry paint on canvas
51 x 66cm

The minibus dumped us in a Sainsbury's carpark early on Friday night. The banter died. No one spoke as we pulled on our tabards and attached our identity badges. In silence, we fastened the forms to our clipboards and checked we had our pens. We held up our phones to show Tansy they were switched on. As she gave us our instructions, she raised her fist over her chin like an invisible megaphone. I'd hoped we would get the seafront, but Tansy gave it to Ambi and Adam. An occasional catalogue model and a county level gymnast, they were the team's most attractive personalities. Tansy always handed them the most promising runs.

It had been rammed into us that no one gives to a charity. They give to you. To succeed, you have to be a charismabot with all the latest gizmos and gadgets. Tansy had instilled in us that deep down we all have the same pluck, persistence and charm as Ambi and Adam. We hadn't failed if we didn't look great in a miniskirt, or couldn't hang upside down like a giant blonde bat. It was more about conviction than appearance. It was a question of belief. I needed to keep working on my belief.

Maybe Tansy could inspire us because she didn't want to be anything else. She had quit her Drama degree after a fully committed tabard hustling for Cancer Research outside a TK Maxx in Hull utterly wowed her with his passion. She'd known straightaway she was a street fundraiser.

Marysia, my street buddy, she still thought she was going to be a singer-songwriter, next year's Laura Marling. Some svengali of the neo-folk scene would soon discover her. She would be perched on a tall stool in a shit pub on the outskirts of Tightfist, plucking her ukulele and singing a song of tender woe. I had seen her play to literally three men and a dog. The dog ran out.

One of our other charismabots, Dangles, he wanted to be a technical juggler. Akhund was punting around a mind, body and spirit textbook that he couldn't describe concisely even to us when we were forced to listen to him on long walks through the towns that time forgot. Whitney wanted to act in the soaps. Tariq wanted to stay at home and smoke weed with Whitney. Rab wanted to smoke weed on his own. Morgy wanted to smoke weed everywhere and Neil wanted to smoke weed and whatever else besides.

Me, I was still waiting for something better to turn up. At least the job made sense to me. I always gave it my best. Otherwise, I'd lose my grip again. Tonight I had one more sign-up to hit my target. Whatever the weather, whatever the flack, I was going to get it.

'Go out and save the world,' said Tansy. 'And remember, I know where you are.' She tapped her smartphone with her thumb ring. Her GPS app would be tracking our movements via our phones.

Marysia and I made sure we looked extra-energetic as we strode across the carpark. Once out of sight, we dawdled like schoolkids on a Monday morning. The town was dank, the light beginning to fade already. It was still September. It felt much later in the year.

'Put it this way,' I said, 'if we'd got the seafront I'd get my last sign for sure. You'd break your duck. I'm not bitter about it. You bitter?'

Marysia stopped on the pavement. Under her tabard, her long army surplus Parka hid her short skirt. With her legs bare she looked naked under her coat again. There was a ukulele hidden somewhere in that coat.

'I can't shine as the face of famine tonight,' she said.

'It's not a famine. It's a flood.'

'It's food shortages caused by a flood. And who cares, it's Friday night in Bedrock. I'm going to go home and cry and I want to die. I can't do it tonight, Theo.'

I took my phone out and waggled it in her face.

'We're on-track, we can't bunk. Tansy's like the Eye of Sauron.'

'Conformist.'

'Exhibitionist.'

'Traditionalist.'

'Second rate Fifi Geldof who thinks she's Patti Smith.'

'Fuck off, Seventh Day Adventist.'

'You heard Tansy, we've got to put food in the mouths of little kids.'

'I wish I could actually put food in the mouths of little kids, not knock on doors and get called a chugger.'

'You are a chugger. You less OK than usual?'

'No. Let's get on with it.'

We linked our elbows and walked.

'I chug. You chug,' I said.

'He chugs. She chugs,' said Marysia.

'We chug. You chug.'

'They chug. They chug.'

I chug, that's what I do. Tansy and lots of others in the £2.69 a month game hate the C-word. Chugger. Charity Mugger. What we do is not mugging. Do you think, standing there all uppity and afraid, that asking you to help the world's most unfortunate people by giving less than you spend on a loaf and a pint of milk is like being violently assaulted by a desperate, underprivileged individual in a ski mask?

I don't find the C-word offensive. I'll use it to my advantage if I can. When I come to your door, I'll ignore how out of joint and edgy you look. I'll say, 'Hey, don't worry. I'm not Jehovah's Witnesses. Now, those cranks do believe that the end of the world is nigh, but we at International Bridge, we're here to help others survive the end.'

I'm your friendly neighbourhood chugger, here to help you do your bit for the victims of earthquakes, drought, hurricanes, tsunami and floods like the one Team Tansy were raising funds for tonight.

The Ganges had burst its banks in the delta region of Bangladesh. A thousand people were dead already and twenty million without food or homes. High water had taken out their villages and their crop. I was here to help others save them from the end of their world.

We crossed a deserted high street where a web of bunting spun around on the breeze. The tarmac shimmered with recent rain. A dozen or so young men swarmed out of a pub called The Hero of Copenhagen. We didn't chug them. No point. In town centres, you see more people but you get blanked most of the time, especially after the shops have shut. Yes, you need to be persistent and you need to be emotional, but you also need to be selective. These guys were whooping like Aztecs. We crossed the road to avoid them.

According to Tansy, only one in a thousand people are amenable to signing-up. If you can approach a thousand people a day, seven hundred will ghost you; and a hundred will tell you just what they think of you, your occupation, your morals, your tabard or the people you're asking them to help. Another hundred will spin you some line as to why they can't give that will be so surreal you'll start to think you're being punked by a TV prank show. Ninety-five will try to fob you off with cash you can't accept, and then get angry with you for not taking their shrapnel and pocket fluff. Four lumbering ghouls will offer you sex al fresco.

Among all these raindrops will be a single glitter of gold.

I'd had four glitters that week, Marysia none. We were supposed to get five each. I wasn't going to give up tonight until I'd snatched my number five from the drizzle. Our instructions were to explore a residential district to the south.

A more affluent area, the residents there could be more willing to let us pitch.

We left the town centre and scampered through a housing estate that seemed abandoned to silence. We didn't even need to discuss whether to go there or not. Beyond a museum of the town's vanished fishing industry, we entered a grid of industrial units. A small, sloping park, purpose-built for proper muggers, funnelled us towards the head of a long terraced street. Cliff tops loomed in the distance. There was a point of light out there.

We agreed to meet at the end. First one to arrive would suffer a punishment dished out by the winner. I took the right side of the street, Marysia the left. I drew three blanks with my first three knocks. One of the houses was lit up like Las Vegas but no one came to the door. I got my first 'fuck off chugger' on my fourth house. Marysia must have had a pitch at this point. She was behind me. I was heading for oblivion at the end of the street. She'd never won this game. I suspected she'd stored up some terrible reckoning for me.

At the fifth house I was allowed to pitch to a woman who'd had so much collagen plungered into her lips that she looked like a rudimentary prototype for a new budget range of blow-up doll.

She didn't give money to brown people. She slammed the door.

When I described the flood to one of her neighbours she told me it was 'their' fault for breeding so much. Another said he would give if the money were to build an ark but not to pay bureaucrats, lefties and twats like me. Next I got a man who just let me pitch and pitch and pitch and then said he was a ward of court and not in control of his own bank account. He was about fifty.

A house where a rhythm of dull thuds came from inside wobbled my innards on the garden path until I thought better of it and left.

Marysia was still behind me on the other side of the road. I sent her a text telling her she was a dirty chugger. She sent me one back saying I was a Maoist and a harpist.

We both drifted towards and away from houses full of ghosts.

Sorry.

Sorry.

Sorry.

No.

No.

Fuck off.

No.

We're eating.

We're knackered.

My son's just died.

I would love to help but you see I've got to pay for this new cybernetic eyeball thing that I used to be able to get on prescription and they now say it going to cost fourteen grand and I don't have fourteen grand.

Disabled.

Potless.

Victim of cuts.

Benefit of clergy.

We're Jehovah's Witnesses, you misrepresent our beliefs.

It's not the end of the world. It's God's will.

I don't give to Africa.

I don't give a flying fuck where it is. We're with Nigel.

SLAM.

Behind me, I could hear Marysia's distinctive three-rap knock on the other side of the street getting nearer as she did her thing. We were almost aligned now. Her failure of charisma was catching up with my flagging charm. She was slightly ahead of me when I thought I'd found my sparkle in the rain.

A guy came to the door, a beardy, skinny Shaggy-out-of-*Scooby Do* lookalikey. I told him that I was his friendly neighbourhood chugger. He laughed, rubbed his nose and asked me in. His front room still had a Christmas tree up. Fairy lights smeared the otherwise dark walls with pink and blue spangles. A massive TV was connected to an old skool VCR. He'd freeze-framed a scene from one of my least favourite films, *2001: A Space Odyssey*. An extra in a monkey suit must have just chucked a bone up into the air. The bone was hanging in the sky, suspended, like it was never going to come down again.

Shaggy and I had a proper real live human discussion about whether *2001* is actually any good. I've always considered it unwatchable bollocks but had to admit that I'd never seen any further than the extras in monkey suits chucking bones at the beginning. Shaggy told me that I needed to hang on in there and keep an open mind, go with the cosmic flow. That big black slab the monkeys find, that's us, man. That's what's going to do for us. It's coming back one day to put us in a zoo where we belong. And 2001's got that bloke who used to be in *Rising Damp* playing a Russian cosmonaut. They don't do things like that anymore, the people who make films. They play safe nowadays. None of the little wankers from *The Inbetweeners* are in *Interstellar*.

Shaggy asked me if I wanted a coffee and I said, yeah, I'll have a coffee, milk no sugar, plenty of caffeine, but then he paused and said, 'Hey, you're wearing a badge.' I told him I was from International Bridge and I'd been talking to his neighbours about how they can save the children of Bangladesh from the end of their world. And Shaggy just looked at me and said, all quiet and forlorn, 'So you don't want any gear then?'

No glitter. Only rain.

I heard Marysia before I caught up with her. She was sitting on the garden wall of the last house on the left, plucking random chords from her ukulele. The street doglegged towards the sea. Opposite was a break in a hedge, a stile, black fields sloping upwards. Above them, the light on the cliff glimmered. There was a cluster of buildings on the cliff.

'I claim my prize,' I said.

'You got one?'

'No, but the night is young.'

'It's not, it's already being swindled out of its pension.'

'One day I'll tell you a story about that sort of thing.'

'Go on then. I need cheering up.'

'Nah. I won this run, though, and for my prize, can I be excused coming to your gig tomorrow? I can't do it anymore.'

'I can't do *this* anymore.'

'Oh c'mon. It's not your fault.'

'I know it's not my fault.'

'I like to think that if someone doesn't gives to a charity they give to you, when they don't give to you they don't give to the charity.'

'People hate the charities *and* they hate me. They want a Bargain Bucket and Taylor Swift.'

'There's a thousand songs in a street full of losers.'

'I don't have your unflappable sass. These people are hideous. This is horrible ...'

Yes, it was horrible, but not as horrible as famine. Marysia was always like this at the end of every run, not only the tough ones. She was like it at the beginning, like it at the end. She hadn't been doing it as long as me. In my first few months, at the end of every day I'd had to take a long look at myself. I needed to drop away, find an emotional space I called the Decompression Chamber.

In my previous career I used to enter a similar place, the Floatation Tank. As I floated I didn't have any explanation for my behaviour or any idea of what lived beyond the sensations and tilt.

'Maybe I'll have a word with Tansy,' I said. 'It was maybe misjudged to come here on a Friday night.'

'Misjudged?' Who are you now? The strategy simulator? That's it. I'm going off-track.'

'We've got two hours left. She'll know.'

'Bollocks to you for not coming to my gig. Bollocks to Tansy, stupid cow.'

Marysia took out her phone, slipped off the casing and removed the SIM. She held out her arm and dropped the SIM into the drain.

'Bit drastic,' I said.

'Jurist.'

'Defeatist.'

My phone blipped. Tansy had sent me a text. 'Can you see Marysia? She's off-track.'

'See?' I said.

'I quit,' said Marysia.

'No you don't. We're in this together.'

'We're not. You don't even like my songs.'

'I'll come to the gig. You're better than Fifi Geldof, easily. And Bob Geldof couldn't have done better than you here tonight. I'll tell Tansy you've lost your phone and you're with me.'

'I'm going.'

'No, you're not, you're coming with me.'

'No, you're coming with me. We're going to hit the front, sneer at some frightening people, smash up a pub and then vandalise the train back.'

'I'll see you at the minibus then?'

'Cock to the minibus, where you going?'

'The houses up there. I reckon that's where the richer ones live.'

'I don't care.'

'Please, Marysia, I don't want you to quit on anything.'

She pulled up her hood and walked off towards the seafront. I stood and watched, torn between heading out for signature number five and going after her. I was just about to cross when I saw Marysia heading back up the road.

'I'm scared,' she said.

'Catastrophist.'

'Sophist.'

We trudged across a sodden field towards the light on the cliff. The moon was full and high. Tankers shimmered out at sea. Birds screeched and chittered in the soft darkness. Marysia was certain that she'd quit for good this time. I told her that I didn't think there was a living in playing the ukulele. Too many quirky fuckers are doing four-string cover versions of nineties R 'n' B hits or Ace of Base numbers. She should find another instrument, like the xylophone or the serpent. She'd stand out from the crowd then.

'Annexationist,' she said.

We came to a property surrounded by a fence and trees that rustled in the dark. A two-storey wooden house was tacked on to a barn. Light shone from a ground floor window.

'I'm not going in there,' said Marysia. 'We're not coming out if we go in there.'

'Probably just a bed and brekkie for refinery workers or something. You want to stay out here in the dark?'

'Better the darkness you know.'

'Don't be a wombat.'

'I've quit, remember. You chug. I don't chug.'

'I'll be five minutes.'

'Yeah, right.'

To give the residents warning, I let the gate swing so it cracked against the post behind me. The light drifted from between the curtains of the largest window on the ground floor. Level with the front of the house now, I could see a gravel pathway flanked by black oaks. It led to the cliff and the moon out at sea. I knocked on the door, twice, hard, but I hoped not in an ominous way. Behind me, Marysia's ukulele twanged twice then stopped as soon as the door opened.

A meaty middle-aged woman in a wide-belted Tyrolean skirt stood before me. Her lips trembled. Her watering eyes seemed for an instant to swarm with stars. Just as I was beginning to feel as if I'd intruded – I am a professional intruder, outcome-orientated and immune to shame – she half-curtsied, almost stumbled.

'Hey, don't be scared,' I said. 'I'm not Jehovah's Witnesses, it's not the end of the world ...'

'Come.'

She grabbed me by the hand and pulled me along a hallway.

I have been to thousands of stranger's houses. If they ask you in, they ask you in. If they waste your time, they waste your time. If they freak you out, you walk away. I was not unsettled, still optimistic, until I noticed the diagrams.

A recurring pattern had been scratched onto the walls in black chalk strokes: two adjacent circles connected by a line and in the middle of that line an offshoot to a distant, smaller circle. I hoped I hadn't blundered into an artists' colony. Artists are always skint but will bollock on for ages.

She paused to open a door.

'We know your name,' she said. 'I am Bernice. Welcome.'

When I first entered that room I felt like I'd walked into a painting I'd seen in a gallery on some school trip where they were trying to teach us about European art and culture and how people in the past were exactly like us, except they wore different clothes for different agendas and customs. All I'd wanted to do was find the café where the local girls hung out, girls who wanted to practise their English, who had never seen a dark-haired boy before. Now I wished I'd listened about the different agendas and customs. These people looked like they came from somewhere else, somewhere removed and abandoned, their clothes, their hair, the fear and wonder in their faces.

Apart from the long wooden table, the room was bare, as if the house had been cleared and they were moving the next day. They all stood up for me, apart from, at the head of the table, a silvery old lady with a severe centre parting. She just stared at me and smiled as if she knew and needed me. Not the usual reaction to your friendly neighbourhood chugger.

She must have realized what I was. She crumpled. Her shoulders shook. She put her head in her veiny hands and started to weep. Beside her, a lithe woman in a brown velvet dress removed her hands from the shoulders of a little girl who could have been her midget twin. She put her arm around the old woman and muttered in her ear. Opposite her, a blonde woman in a lime green jacket and mustard-yellow pleated skirt looked like she'd stepped out of a 1930s advert for a seaside resort. I could imagine her posed against dunes and a sunburst. She put her hand on the old woman's shoulder but kept her eyes fixed on me. I was closest to a short man in a black suit. Slick with Brylcreem and neatly side-parted, his hair was identical to that of a taller man in a grey sharkskin suit across from him. The men reminded me of war-film spies. The short one beamed. The tall one wore a sneer familiar to me in my line of work.

Given the sobbing and the sneer, I realized that I might have arrived at a genuinely bad time.

I wanted to acknowledge this, say I was sorry for barging in, that I would leave them in peace.

All that came out was, 'I'm not Jehovah's witnesses.'

The man in the sharkskin suit relaxed his shoulders and with an elegant swivel of his hips, turned to the trio of women and said, 'Can you not see this is not him?'

The old lady sat up and shrugged the hands from her shoulders.

'Let him speak, Everard.'

'Well, as I was saying, I'm sure you're relieved that I'm not Jehovah's Witnesses and this is not the end of the world. I'd like to say I've been talking to your very generous neighbours, but you guys are the only people out here. Now, I'm pretty sure that you've heard about the flood.'

'The flood,' mouthed the silvery woman.

'You have heard about the flood? That's awesome. And I guess you know how things can only get worse if we don't act, you feel me?'

'The flood has already begun?' said the shorter man.

'It is happening,' said the woman in the mustard skirt.

'It has happened,' I said, 'and now there will only be suffering and hunger and I'm afraid more deaths ...'

'It is to be expected,' said Everard, the taller man.

'But you can help,' I said, 'you can help a lot.'

'Mrs Vita has been trying to help them her whole life. They do not listen.'

'They do not listen,' said the silvery woman, Mrs Vita.

'It's not about their ears, it's about our spirit,' I said. 'We need to have spirit-a-go-go.'

'What is this spirit-a-go-go?' said Everard.

'It's just my fancypants way of saying that we may all feel small and pointless in the face of disaster, but this doesn't need to be the end of their world. We can act. We can help.'

'But it is late,' said Mrs Vita. 'There is little time. How can we make approaches now, when the Time of Closing is so near?'

'Where is it?' said the shorter man.

'In Bangladesh,' I said.

'Bangladesh?'

'He has ways,' said Mustard Skirt.' 'He will take us there.'

'Hey, no one needs to travel,' I said, 'no one needs to get their hands dirty. We'll handle all that. We're the muscle. All you've got to do is find it in your hearts to give just a tiny amount every month, £2.69, same as a little bit of bread and a dash of milk, and with that we can make a huge, huge difference to the children of Bangladesh. Can we count on you here? Can you help?'

Mrs Vita slowly nodded.

'Yes,' they all said, apart from the lithe woman. She was peering at the crown of the little girl's head.

'You are such gorgeous and generous people,' I said. I could already imagine myself bouncing back to the minibus with an extra six signatures, more than double my target. I unfastened a wodge of sign-up forms from my clipboard and swished them about the table. 'Anyone need a pen? I have pens galore?'

There was a thump.

The lithe woman had slammed her fist onto the table.

'We cannot do this. This is unfair. This is cruel. You must tell him.'

'Hey,' I said, 'tell your friendly neighbourhood chugger what?'

No one had reached for the forms.

'We have done everything you asked,' said the lithe woman. 'We cannot do this.'

'You can't give a pint of milk and a loaf of bread a month?'

'We gave it all away.'

'We gave away,' said Mrs Vita, 'all of our material goods.'

'We left our jobs.'

'We sold our houses.'

'In preparation,' said the shorter man, 'for our transportation.'

'To Parataba,' said Mustard Skirt.

'To Parataba,' they all said, even the little girl.

'And now the hour is near,' said the shorter man, 'your craft is in Bangladesh when you made us believe that we needed to greet you here.'

'Because he's not bloody him, is he?' said Everard. 'He's not the Exarch, you cretin.' He turned to me. 'Are you the Exarch?'

I pointed at my badge. 'International Bridge.'

'Perhaps Mrs Vita received the wrong name?' said the shorter man.

'He's not come for us,' said Everard. 'He's one of those bloody chuggers. Tonight of all nights, we get a bloody chugger. Here. The Hour of our Transport. The Time of Closing. We get chugged.'

'There is still time,' said Mrs Vita. 'All is certain. All is written.'

The non-Everard members of the group nodded their agreement. My energy levels sank. My pluck and persistence leaked from my pores. I sat down at the end of the table, opposite Mrs Vita.

'Guys, let's not beat about the bush, you're some sort of cult, right?'

'We prefer alternative religious community,' said Everard.

'I'm feeling you there, mate. I fully understand your problem.'

'You're not the Exarch?' someone said, a woman.

'I knew straightaway he was not the Exarch,' said Everard. 'The Exarch will dress in radiant turquoise, not this unseemly royal blue colour.'

'The Exarch will come,' said Mrs Vita. 'There is still time. And Everard, please be civil to our guest. It is not our way. Dear guest, dear son, what brings you to us, what makes you?'

'You can't believe a word he says,' said Everard. 'They get paid to beg.'

'Please ignore him,' said Mrs Vita. 'You are welcome among the Friends of Parataba.'

'Ladies and gents, this is obviously a special time for you all. I shouldn't be here. Now, if you can just return the forms to me ...'

'There is still time for you while there is still time for us,' said Mrs Vita. 'Tell us, what makes you, what brings you here? We are all guided by strands that connect us to Parataba. We each have ours. You have yours.'

'I told you. I'm rattling the tin for famine relief.

'That we understand. But you have come to us tonight of all nights. It must be written. I ask you not what actions your shell performs here, but what webs orchestrate your shell.'

'She means,' said Everard, 'that it's no little boy's dream to be a chugger.'

'I prefer street fundraiser.'

'You are a good man,' said Mrs Vita. 'No one comes here, and you have come. The Exarch has sent you to us, so you can be with us when he arrives.'

'Are you sure he's coming? I mean ...'

'He doubts,' said Everard. 'The Exarch would not send a doubter.'

'You were all doubters before we met,' said Mrs Vita.

'This world is evil,' said the shorter man. 'The Sink of Corruption. The Font of Decay. We will leave it tonight, for Parataba.'

'Parataba.'

'Parataba.'

Bernice stepped out from behind me and stood next to Mrs Vita.

'Harbinger of Exarch, you have been brought to us by his will, to be with us, The Friends of Parataba, we who have been guided by the Exarch, by his voice and his words as delivered to our Most Honoured Mrs Vita and passed on to us in the ink that he guides to her sacred hands. We, in our last hours here, who await the coming of the Exarch and his craft, his ship of stars that will ferry us to blessed Parataba, we who will live among the Nibunaki, those golden ones who will one day return us to the floodworld to build the new city, the City of Uruanniki that will rise here for the Chosen, we love you, you are one of us now. You are Chosen.'

They all stood up. They each formed a V with their hands that they pressed to their groins. They started to chant; the little girl's voice a squeak just behind the others.

'Parataba, Uruanniki.'

'Parataba, Uruanniki.'

'Parataba, Uruanniki.'

I slammed my palm onto the table.

'I've had enough, this is bollocks, this is nuts. You're not going to do anything stupid here, are you?'

They all froze, turned towards me. No one spoke. For the first time it struck me that I really didn't know where I was or what I was doing. I didn't know who they were and of what they were capable.

From back down along the hallway, down past the chalk patterns that I assumed mapped the Parataba System or described its celestial coordinates, from the outside world came three solid knocks on the door.

Bernice shook as if frazzled by a live current.

'The Exarch of the Nibunaki.'

'The Flood.'

'The Flood.'

'We will be saved from the Flood.'

I knew that knock.

'No, no, no,' I said. 'I can guarantee you, that's not an Exarch.'

'Can I have my twat back?' We heard Marysia trying to get a reaction out of Bernice as they came up the hallway. The door opened. Marysia shuffled into the room. Bernice loomed behind her and stared, crestfallen at Mrs Vita and the Friends of Parataba. They all knitted their fingers and rested them on the table, apart from the little girl. She seemed beguiled by Marysia with her ukulele dangled at hip, giving me the evil eye as if I'd drunk all her lemon vodka and sat on her vinyl copy of Tiger Milk.

'Five minutes, Theo, five minutes. I've been freezing my tits off out there. And there's a weirdo prowling about.'

'The Exarch?' said Everard.

'Does he have a flying saucer?' I said.

'He's probably seeing them, the pissed-up tosser.'

'He's not your man then, Everard.'

Everard shivered. For a second I thought he was going to scream.

'He abandons us and sends another chugger to mock us.'

'Who you calling a chugger, mate?' said Marysia. 'I'm a songstress, with the emphasis on the stress.'

'He understands our situation, Marysia,' I said. 'He's in a cult, but he prefers alternative religious community.'

'This is a cult?' she said.

'The Friends of Parataba. The world's about to end.'

'Coolio. You get them to sign up?'

'They've given away all their worldly goods.'

'Well, Friends of Parrot Tapas,' said Marysia. 'I hope you

find what you're looking for, because sure as donkeybollocks I haven't managed it yet. C'mon, Tee, let's rock the shack before this lot go helter-skelter.'

As I raised myself from my chair, my mobile phone buzzed in my pocket. I ignored it as I gathered my stray forms from the table, glancing up at the Parataba, their folded hands and crushed faces. The little girl fidgeted. She slipped off the lithe woman's lap and gambolled across the room to Marysia. She grabbed hold of the bottom of the ukulele and started to tug at it.

'Look, look, a mini guitar.'

Marysia laughed and crouched down, holding out the ukulele so the girl could stroke it.

'And what's your name?'

The girl paused, as if rummaging her mind to remember.

'Tilly.'

'Well, Tilly, have you ever heard a ukulele?'

Marysia glanced over to the lithe woman. The lithe woman neither flinched nor acknowledged, just kept staring ahead at the woman in the mustard skirt.

Gripping the neck of the ukulele, Marysia swiped its body at my head to shoo me away from my chair. I backed up against the window. She sat down and placed Tilly and the ukulele on her lap. The little girl wriggled and looked up at Marysia with a glee absent from the other faces around the table. Again, the Parataba seemed freeze-framed, two-dimensional. It was as if one part of the table was a photograph and the other a film. I wondered what they would all be doing tomorrow, when their hour had passed, whether they would disband or regroup, how they would live now, rebuild, recover. Lots of the 're' words. Marysia should restyle herself as the singer 'Re'. They could come to her gig tomorrow. It would make it a real post mortem on the post apocalypse.

'Tilly, you comfy?' said Marysia.

'Yes.'

'Do you know what this is called?'

'Ookulele.'

'These are her strings.' She brushed them with a downward stroke of her index fingernail. 'The top one's called G. This is C, this is E and this is A. And a way to remember that is Gay Campers Eat Asparagus.'

'What's asparagus?'

'It's what all the gay campers eat. And these lines at the end are called frets, like to fret is to worry, but the ukulele never worries.'

'I'm not worried. I'm going to Parataba.'

'That's wonderful.' Marysia tilted the ukulele so show Tilly its neck. 'And what you have to do is hold your fingers in a special way on the string by the frets, and pluck the string down here, and you make a chord. This chord is F. See, our fingers here make an F shape.'

Tilly hunched over to look down at the strings as Marysia played *Twinkle, Twinkle, Little Star*. The Parataba didn't notice, in a kind of trance, even Bernice still standing by the door. Marysia played the song again, though this time Tilly sung, her voice small and high, frequently behind the chords. I had been going to rib Marysia that anyone could play that song, even Fifi Geldof. I was going to say, 'Play the hits, Marysia,' but I found myself drawn into the patterns her fingers made as they pressed the frets and how Tilly's little fingers shadowed the patterns. Marysia reached the end of the song. When she tried to take her fingers from the fretboard, Tilly wouldn't let her and kicked her heels against Marysia's shins.

'Can I have another one?'

'OK, as this is the last show on Earth,' said Marysia, 'I'm going to play my new song, just in case, you know, there won't be another time. It's called, "Never Drive Yourself to Dates".'

I was going to ask if it was about the compulsive need to eat a certain type of sickly sweet fruit, but a slow, ponderous rhythm started to prowl around the walls, nine low chords followed by four higher ones, so basslike and deep that I was at a loss as to how she managed to coax the sounds out of the twangy little instrument.

Tilly started to rub her shoulders against Marysia, her feet knocking together with the higher chords. The Parataba did not move or respond, just kept staring straight ahead. The rhythm sped up, gently, ever so slowly gaining pace. It felt like something was coming, lumbering towards the edge of town, drawn to the music, captured by it. The room smelled musty. I wasn't sure if it had always smelled musty or something was wrong with me. I remembered the day I left the law and how all that day I had increasingly felt that the offices smelled of antiseptic, like a hospital, as if they had tried to cover up some underlying, tell-tale stink. I had never quite been able to work out why I had trained to be a lawyer. I didn't know what I wanted to do when I finished uni. I applied for a conversion course because I didn't know what else to do. I ended up training with a firm I'll call Fuckpoor and Munster. I didn't complete the training.

We had been working for a manufacturer of aviation parts disputing a claim for compensation. One of their lifelong employees had contracted mesothelioma, cancer you get from asbestos. After days and days of going over all these old cases, someone finds a ruling where a similar case had been thrown out of court. Bang, party time. I could still feel the slap of the first high five on my palm.

A nasty little feeling rose in my stomach. Something was wrong with me, I knew. I'd misunderstood something, tried to outsmart the one thing you can't outsmart: the way things are.

Marysia used her little finger to draw another, more delicate, shimmery rhythm as counterpoint to the baseline. Her fingers started to blur as the song burst forth into a much faster version of the initial movement, as if it has been winding up its gears and was now buzzing around our heads like some manic clockwork bird. I was trying to think through the earlier parts of this evening, the walk from the carpark and through the town, along the horrible street and over the dark fields, following the light and the patterns in black chalk to this room, these people. That and all before it seemed to have happened at the same unsustainable pace as this music. Walking in circles. Walking the grid. Lying on the floor of my old flat, drunk at nine thirty on a work night, headphones on in the floatation tank, slow, drone music to keep me still and in place.

The popping of a champagne cork and being high-fived by a woman called Emma Lau. I don't blame Emma. She was merely swept along by the way things are, but her touch had sent me on my walk across the open plan office and down the stairs and across the foyer, the square and the city to my flat, and then, after issues with landlords and credit card companies out again to walk the streets of the towns that time forgot.

I wondered about the Friends of Parataba, how each of them would have had an Emma Lau moment, something that would have made them look up and never look down or sideways again.

The lithe woman must have given in to the music. She was grinning at Tilly now, as if something had made her realize who Tilly was, Tilly with her fingers shadowing Marysia's. Marysia kept adding new sounds to the music, extra chords, surprising riffs. All of the Parataba now, all except for Mrs Vita were turned to Tilly and smiling. The lithe woman and Mustard Skirt were tapping their palms on the table. Everard and the shorter man tapped their palms, too, and then started to stamp their feet. When they started to stamp their feet, I stamped, too. I was stamping along as the music grew faster and faster, as if something was coming, something was going to appear.

The little girl swung her legs and wriggled side to side. Marysia squinted and bit her bottom lip and let the chords speed up and up and up until it looked like the music sucked the breath out of her, the music would shatter the instrument.

She released her fingers from the fretboard.

She stood up and lofted the ukulele with one hand, dragged Tilly in front of her waist with the other.

'And that, my friends,' she panted, 'is the end. I'm not fat, so I didn't sing. Thank you. Thank you all.'

'Oh my,' said the shorter man, startled like he'd been shaken awake. 'The time.'

The Parataba stood up at once.

'The time has passed, Mrs Vita,' said Mustard Skirt.

'Seven minutes, thirty-eight seconds ago' said the lithe woman.

Bernice looked like she was about to faint, or explode.

'The flood? We are flooded.'

The shorter man barged me aside and pulled back the curtains. He opened the window. The night breezed into the room.

'Not again,' he said.

I don't know for exactly how long we all stood there in silence. I tried to avoid looking at Marysia. If I'd looked at Marysia, and Marysia had looked at me, we were going to make each other laugh. I'm not sure if laughing would have made us more human or less. We stood there in silence until Mrs Vita told everyone to wait outside while she attempted to commune with the Nibunaki from the planet Parataba.

Bernice's breathing was now so laboured that it was sensible to take her outside for air. The woman in the mustard skirt helped her into the hallway, followed by the shorter man and the lithe woman holding Tilly by the hand. We followed Everard, who had the slow, dignified gait of a man following an emperor's coffin on a gun carriage. Marysia grabbed my elbow just inside the hallway.

'These people are insane,' she whispered.

'That song was insane. You been taking lessons?'

'We can't leave, Theo. They might and cut their own knackers off.'

'I don't think they're like that.'
'It's a flippin' doomsday cult.'
'Alternative religious community.'
'They've got a little kid'.
'Look, let's hang about until we know Tilly is safe.'
'What about the Eye of Sauron?'
I checked my phone. Six texts from Tansy and three missed calls.
'I'll text her something has come up.'
'We mustn't let them out of our sight. There's a cliff out there.'
'They're not lemmings.'
'They are.'

We followed the path alongside the house and caught sight of The Friends of Parataba as they trudged down a slope towards the cliff's edge. We already could hear the placid slosh of waves. The moon was at its highest point. It shimmered its trail upon the sea. Out there, too, were red pinpricks and the glittering lights of shipping and rigs. There was no rain, only the dank autumn breeze. Nothing in nature was angry with any of us.

'How are we going to get home?' said Marysia.
'Flying saucer.'

When we caught them up, the Friends were in loose formation, close to the edge. Tilly let go of her mother's hand and ran to Marysia. Marysia gave her the ukulele. Tilly zigzagged around on the grass before collapsing on her bottom. She started to throw her palms at the strings. The shrill plinking sounds bothered no one. The other Friends were all staring at the sea, at the moonshine and glimmers. None of them spoke to us. We didn't speak to each other. I wanted to hold Marysia's hand but I didn't want Marysia to hold my hand. Maybe I just wanted to hold something.

I felt terrified, but not for them. They knew, or had faith that they understood something certain about the world. I wondered just when Mrs Vita had started to believe the voices she heard in her head, and how she managed to attract and convince each of them that when the world ended only they would be saved. I wondered if I had ever heard these voices, in the Floatation Tank, in the Decompression Chamber, walking the streets. Had Emma Lau and Tansy and Marysia, Shaggy and all of them down there, had we all chosen to block the voices out?

It would seem that the end had come before. Mrs Vita had promised the end. It had not come. The end was still ahead of them, out there, shifting and shimmery, like the twinkle the moon gave to the waters.

Between endings, they were still special.

The random twangs of the ukulele stopped. We all must have felt that we were being watched. We turned around. The Friends of Parataba turned from the sea. Tilly was standing alongside Mrs Vita. Mrs Vita held up in the pinch of her fingers sheets of paper that fluttered on the breeze.

'There has been a message,' she said. 'The Nibunaki have spared the other's world tonight. They have been moved by the goodness of our guests, these good people here. The Nibunaki do not wish to harm such people. While such people are as they are, doing what they do, they will not raise the waters.' She gestured at us. 'Should that change, another date will be decided and the flood will surely come.'

'Bloody chuggers.'

The voice came from behind me, but I could have been talking to myself.

CROW
AIDEN O'REILLY

The End 'Crow' (2015)
Gloss and masonry paint on canvas
51 x 66cm

Sharon Ganley straightened up from the window box. Out of the corner of her eye she noticed the livery of a DHL van. The driver angled an elbow out the side window and scrutinised each house door. He winked at her with the general licence of tradespeople to push at PC boundaries.

'Grand day for it,' he called out. 'How's that Seramat working for you?'

It took her a second to figure out what he meant. A twist stepper waist-trimmer with built-in heart monitor, delivered two weeks ago. She had no car, and relied on online shopping. The driver must have an excellent memory. Or more plausibly he delivered for only a small circle of companies.

'Just fine,' she said. 'Anything for me today?'

'Ehh, no.' He slowed to a stop, dipped his head and rummaged. 'Ms Ganley. No.' He leaned back in the seat.

'Time for a break?'

'More or less. Just figuring out where to go next.' He rubbed an eyebrow. He had the look of someone starved for conversation.

'It's all go,' said Sharon.

'Ha. Do you know what it is?' He waited for her eyes to meet his gaze. 'I only do this for the fun of it. What's in the back there?' He jerked a thumb. 'Could be empty and I'd still drive around. Chatting to people. Admiring the scenery.' The van moved off. A clenched fist protruded from the side window.

Sharon waved faintly at the departing vehicle. Thank God for whimsical people, she thought, wouldn't life be boring without them.

She snipped a few stems from the window box and considered an arrangement against her palm. She prided herself on avoiding the two sinkholes that suck in mothers with grown children: cats, and reality TV. Sometimes she would browse through cat discussion forums just to see the depths to which such mania could lead.

The phalanx of trees at the end of the road blocked the sun from Sharon's front garden. Even now, flecked with May buds, the trees looked sinister. Mere sun-thieves, Sharon hated them. But nothing to be done – one cannot petition the local council to have a chainsaw applied to eighty-year-old chestnut trees.

Stop staring at me, Mister Goddamn Crow. The crow was perched on the whip-end of a branch. It wasn't just perched; its claws gripped tenaciously to the bare switch as it dipped and shivered.

Fly fly away, she aimed a thought at the implacable bird, *and go stare at some other bored parent, grown child, too much time on her hands. Go away you transmogrified fragment of a broken umbrella.* The crow obligingly took to its wings, only to glide down to the ground. It pecked at the gravel, scratched with a foot, and pecked again.

The second-youngest McGuin child (was he still in training pants?) toddled past the front gate holding a double 99. Not yet five and he could be seen wandering the road at all hours. The child's lips quivered with the mental strain of maintaining equilibrium with the confection.

'Size of you and that ice cream. Mind you don't trip over and drown in it.'

The McGuin family did not lack the usual prole necessities of Xbox, iPad, and smartphones. But they never had spare cash, and certainly none to give to the second-littlest McGuin.

'Where'd you get the money for that?'

'The ice cream man is giving them out.'

'Is he gone mad or what?'

Mrs McGuin appeared at her front door.

'There's your mammy looking for you.' The child did not

turn his head. Neither did Joan McGuin cast a glance up or down the street.

A car sped down from the roundabout. It was going too fast for this residential area. It jerked to a halt in the middle of the road outside the McGuin's. Three of the four doors swung open and a bass beat escaped. Joan McGuin approached a few steps, stopped, and proceeded to exchange excited shrieks with the driver. Her son, apparently, from the way he tagged an urgent *Ma* onto each sentence. Mrs McGuin disappeared back inside momentarily, emerged clutching several empty bags, and got in beside her son. The doors slammed shut and the beat choked off. The car accelerated uncertainly, veering from one side to the other before finding a straight line. A brief illusion of silence followed.

April sixteenth, she checked on the calendar inside. No bank holiday, no mega-gig at the stadium. After zapping a pod through the Dolce Gusto she reassured herself there was nothing very unsettling about a delivery driver with too much time on his hands, and another emergency afflicting Joan McGuin.

'You mean you heard absolutely *nothing*?' Her daughter Josephine flexed her nose indignantly.

'I'm *busy* with things. And if I do get a moment to myself, I sit at the computer and do my scheduling.' Scheduling was the term she used for the online promo she did for a chiropractic practice.

'So anyway, it's not like I'm going to just drop out of school and stare at the wall?' Josephine trailed after her mother. 'Mother? You're worried I might become a rock star and get like zippers in my cheek?'

'Mum' had been abandoned in recent months. Josephine needed a parental figure to rebel against. It exhausted Sharon; she wasn't much suited to being authoritarian.

'Oh dear I hope not.'

'Mother? Will you stop being *busy*.'

'This morning young McGuin went by with a big ice cream in his hand.'

Josephine's eyes widened beautifully.

'My God, mother. You have the ability to say such *amazingly* absolutely pointless *junk*.'

The doorbells chimed their descending fifths. Sharon set down the paring knife and wiped her hands. When she reached the front door there was no one there. The same crow still clenched the same branch. All craw and claw and pitched wings. Three art-student types walked by at a clip, one holding a chihuahua in a tartan jacket, another a guitar. Flitters of their conversation reached Sharon's ears.

'... monster trucks crashing into each other all day'

'... full tank of petrol and autocruise'

'... wait till she sees this, hey!'

The trio marched swiftly out of sight. Sharon felt a hush in the air, as though a large item of machinery somewhere distant had powered off. Then sounds of vehicles revving, distant clamour, a thin scent of engine fumes. She closed the door.

'Jo,' she called. 'What was the news?' While her daughter yammered inconclusively, she switched on the radio.

Traffic backed up on all radial routes … *contraflow in operation … we haven't witnessed scenes like this since the fall of the Berlin wall … back to Jason Cotter in the newsroom. This morning's announcement has discombobulated a lot of people yes Karen it's a real word here at QT city we are recommending you just carry on, yeah, have fun and carry on or be terrified and carry on … no parking space at Chiswick Mall …*

Josephine's voice was low and reverent. 'There's been a *Guardian* feed all morning. People are tuning to their radios like in olden times. There were queues at all the shops when I was on …'

'Jesus Christ, why didn't you say so earlier? Call a taxi. No, we'll have to walk.' Sharon stooped to the storage space and rooted out bags – heavy-duty supermarket bags, tote bags, rolls of black plastic.

'They say not to panic, Mum. They say everything's gonna be alright.'

'Of course they're going to say that. Come on, get proper shoes on you, get those hiking boots you have.'

Traffic, both human and vehicular, proceeded slowly up the N8. The crowd exuded the nervous energy of a football mob in hostile territory. Abandoned cars blocked the hard shoulder. Some contained passed-out teenagers.

'Look,' said Josephine. A double-decker bus crawled along the fast lane. It was crammed full with young people, singing and cheering. 'Look, Mum, the driver.' Three teenagers were squeezed into the driver's booth. It was hard to distinguish which one held the steering wheel.

A sound of heavy jogging behind them, Josephine cried out and was flung headlong to the pavement. The group of youngsters in tracksuits stopped. The one with a party keg on his shoulder set it down.

'Are you OK? Sorry, sorry, I didn't see you.' The young man helped Josephine to her feet. 'I'm really sorry, I was focussed straight ahead. Are you OK?'

Josephine smiled through gritted teeth.

'God I feel so stupid about this,' said the young man. He apologised again a couple of times and caught up with his friends. Sharon wondered how much longer such politeness would last.

An hour later and exhaustion began to hit them. The litre bottles of water in their bags tore into their shoulders. And now the citybound lanes were clogging up too. Cars with bags and boxes pressed up against the windows, roofrack loads tied down with rope. Traffic edged forward nervously. A couple of rangy men stood smoking at the opposite verge. With no car, no bags, and no houses within an hour's walk, they had no legitimate reason to be there.

A car slowed and a female voice shouted at them. Sharon stared at the woman, confused. 'They want to give us a lift, come on,' said Josephine. The woman made a thumb gesture to the rear. The door lock pins popped. Josephine opened the door, and a few moments later they were ensconced in the comforting scent of taxi vanilla.

'You looked totally jaded there, the pair of you,' laughed the woman. Her boyfriend threw a grin back at them. 'Have you been on the road long?'

'Two, maybe three hours,'

'Oh my god. That's *awful*. Look, it's loosening up ahead, isn't it, Mason? Twenty minutes and we'll be there.'

'Do you think there'll be much left? Any tinned food, pasta, rice?'

The woman glanced back. 'Well we're not driving all this way just for *that*.'

'What are you buying then?'

'I love the Kenzo stuff. Louis Vuitton travel cases, one of those Bamix blenders for the kitchen, a Gore-Tex jacket for yours truly.'

'I thought … Isn't there a state of emergency? The news … We just rushed out.'

Mason spoke up. 'Uhh, it's not actually officially a state of emergency. Apparently.' He groped with his left hand in the space behind the handbrake. 'There's a newspaper there. At a crisis like this we have to give a show of confidence. We just want to be there. Even if it's just a coffee and pastry. We're not going to let this thing bring us down.'

'Far from it,' his girlfriend/partner chimed in.

Sharon opened out the newspaper. Josephine beside her closed her eyes and slouched.

> … In a field which has not seen any advance since nineteen thirty-six, philosophers across the world were taken aback at yesterday's announcement from Durham. It appears the full significance was not at first appreciated. News of the result was exchanged by email for several

hours before any media channel picked up on it ...

... this conclusion, or discovery as others would have it, refutes all naïve concepts of free will and purpose. This makes Nihilism as irrefutable as gravity, or evolution, or the existence of Australia. This is the Higgs Boson moment for Nihilism. If John Gray were alive he'd be dancing the tango. Or maybe weeping that nobody will bother buying his books of what have suddenly become 'mere speculations in the dark'.

... Darran Kyberd, one of the original team. 'We had no idea it would be such a game changer. We were working to a deadline, checking references, then one of the editors asks can he cite it in a talk he's giving, next thing I know, people are telling me, get on Twitter, get on Twitter now.

'I don't know,' said Sharon. 'I need to get home. I'm tired, I can't ... There could be trouble. Chaos on the streets.'

'That's the thing,' Mason said resolutely, almost angrily. 'We don't let it get to us. We party on. We keep things moving on. This – this! is what the nihilists dread to see.' Mason slowed the car to take the entrance ramp into the mall carpark. 'People shopping, and being perfectly content and fulfilled doing so.'

Sharon powered on the laptop and a moment of reverie was forced upon her as the boot screen turned baby blue. The mall had been exhausting, but at least Josephine had enjoyed it. Her daughter had run into several friends there and swapped epic stories of where they had been when they first heard the news. Sharon had been dragged from boutique to boutique all afternoon.

She logged on to her work content manager. Her work involved not just scheduling patients, but also promoting the chiropractor's practice on social media and sending out sms reminders. Not much activity today. Perhaps everyone was out partying, or responding to the news in some other manner of their choice.

A sequence of red flickers through the louvre blinds caught her attention. She went out to the front door and stood for some time with one hand on the front gate. Flickers again, filtered through the spidery phalanx of trees. She felt a surge of anxiety, and then the corona of a firework mushroomed above the trees. The crackle arrived a few seconds later. Sounds of distant sirens.

Back inside the house was quiet. Maybe too quiet. She padded up the stairs and gave her daughter's door a gentle knock before opening. The humped profile of Josephine on the bed shifted a fraction. The window behind her glowed sodium orange from streetlamps. As a child, Josephine had never needed a night light.

'You OK, Jo?'

'Yeah.'

'Want a cup of that melissa-something tea?'

'No, I'm fine.' Josephine turned from the window and sat up. The quilt fell off her – she hadn't actually been under it, she was just holding it around herself.

'Don't be worried, Mum. Really.'

'Worried about what?'

'I was just daydreaming. I wasn't thinking about anything.'

'Can I turn on the light then?'

'Sure. Yeah, turn it on.'

Josephine was right. There was something about the intimacy of radio that made it suited to the day. Sharon moved the kitchen radio into her home office area and switched through the channels.

... major fluctuations all morning, weakening of leading indicators, except in east Asia which was barely affected. But tomorrow is another dawn, and markets are free floating, not free falling as many had feared ⁴⁴⁴⁴ *We have Frain Lynch on the line. What's the impact on the elections, Frain? Hi Mortimer good to be here. We anticipate a triumph of personality over policy that's something the smarter candidates will bear in mind* ⁴⁴⁴⁴ *this absence, this void, it's been hinted at for years. But you know, how do you analyse what isn't there?* ⁴⁴⁴⁴ *dancing Mortimer. Dancing.*

The emphatic treble of the voices annoyed her. She switched off the radio and clicked back on to her scheduling interface. She ticked off cells to create a provisional timetable for the coming month. She browsed through the customer database and composed personal reminders. She performed internet searches on influential clients. There were a thousand little things to do to keep this day in place. And as she clicked and tabulated, her awareness of her surroundings dwindled. Her back was stiff from being in the one position, her legs tingled from being still for too long, but she did not notice these things. She was immersed in the minutiae of work almost totally – apart from a low-lying anxiety, a lurking tangle of thought that was on its way to becoming a headache rather than a thought. A headache of anxiety that she was only what she appeared to be. Her daughter was grown up and soon would leave for college, this freelance job too would not last, her old friends had moved out of contact – she had reason to feel anxious, but these were not the reasons. And as she clicked and scanned she understood that only a small fraction of her mind was engaged in the work, and the larger part was battling constantly against this anxiety, thought-forms joining battle on her behalf. And she knew that if she acknowledged these as her own, she was truly lost. So she sought to turn aside. Turn aside, and sink into unfolded unreflection, to be this only now what she does and no other, and the clicking went on and the chatting would go on and the flower arranging would go on, but in rooms all over the city, the lights were dimming one by one.

Some day soon, the paradigm of decision and emotion will become, not that of the mechanical songbird, nor yet the order of myriad pulses on a metallic printed surface, but that of a crow that pecks and scratches, stares with a clear eye, and pecks and scratches again.

SOULS
MICHAEL CROSSAN

The End 'Souls' (2015)
Gloss and masonry paint on canvas
51 x 66cm

On a dead road, the sedan cruised mooncast. Sleek into the wind slap. Backseat the commandant watched a pearl horizon. Clean sky on the Tatras. He leaned his forehead against the window and thinked a boyhood time in Rathen. Fireside talkers. Elders aglow. His father preachy on nature and Saxony and God. Pious sayings about the Elbe peaks.

'Heaven's spires, my hole,' the commandant whispered, and his breath dusted the glass and buried his view.

Big miles uphill, nighttime fell whiter. Off a crag bend the sedan steered onto a dirt track. Bumped over potholes and stones and branches and log parts. He glared at the rear-view mirror. 'Slower, Jan.'

'Sorry, Herr Commandant.' The chauffeur braked and down-geared and the car crept, headlamps on full beam, illuminating the path.

'Do not say commandant. I am Kazimiers Kapka.'

'Yes,' the chauffeur said, a nod at the mirror.

'Who am I?'

'You are Kazimiers Kapka.'

'My papers say so.'

'You are the architect.'

'And you are Jan Domarski. My secretary. You are not Jepp Bonhof, the commandant's chauffeur. You are no more him.'

'I forget it. I am all the time scared.'

'Papers say who you are. Your identification tells it.'

'I am Jan Domarski.'

'Good. I say always, Jan. You say always, Mr Kapka.'

'Yes.'

'Yes who?'

'Yes, Mr Kapka.'

'Yesterday you near miss a ditch. Tonight you miss my identity. Wake up, Jan. Shake your skull.'

The trail carved through forestry. Naked hag woods. Firs frostcoat. A cliff turn and downhill the trail opened and smoothed and the chauffeur shifted gear and the sedan moved fiercer and truer. The commandant tapped the glass partition. 'That is strange,' he said, watching lights blink through shrubbery.

Heavier into the valley the chauffeur said, 'It is streetlights.'

'Strange, no, Jan.'

'No place is here. Not on any map I know.'

'Could be Zakopane.'

'I am twelve miles to Zakopane.'

'What is here? On the map.'

'Old roads are here. And the forest. I know the map.'

'I see a street. There look. It is not a village. Only a street.'

'No place here is on the map.'

'The electrics work. Funny, that.'

'I don't know.'

'Funny tricks, Jan.'

Lights formed larger and brighter. The commandant handswept his greased hair and read a sign on a building. HOTEL. Lit neon. A beacon burn. Fixed vertical on the slab above entrance doors. He scanned the building. Broad and tall and dull and cracked. Time tired. Like a jail wing of some relic castle. 'Looks like the viper den. Do you remember there, Jan?'

'I remember that hotel.'

'Bolshevik swine burned it.'

'This place looks like there. It is not on the map.'

'For us it is luck. I am everywhere sore. Two nights sleep on this seat has killed my arse.'

'You are strong. A bull man.'

'My bones need a bed.'

'A bed will be good.'

'It is luck, Jan. I always have it.'

'A lucky hotel.'

'Yes.' The commandant lit a cigarette with a chubby steel lighter. He inhaled and thought about the girl he too soon gave to the chimney. The black hair Serbian. He fire thinked her. Liked thinking his shouts at her. Liked remembering touching her skin. Tasting her warmth. Playing with her as he liked when he foul spun. 'A lucky hotel,' he said, seeing the place closer, his nose pouring smoke. He opened his wallet and unzipped a pocket and stroked the Serbian girl's hair part.

Turning off the trail into the street, rain hit the window screen. The chauffeur switched the wipers on fast. Rain hit quicker and blacker and the street was messy visible and HOTEL ragged like a flame.

Parked kerbside the rain stopped. They close saw the building. The many windows were curtain kept. Shone black as the wet granite. Lamplight blasted entrance glass doors. Yellow spread on steps. Faint lay on the pavement. There was no people movement. There was only the sign and doorway light.

'Do not speak here,' the commandant said, and flattened his coat lapels and tidied his tie, sorting his civilian wear and mind. 'I will talk. I say the language easy.'

'I will not talk, Mr Kapka.' The chauffeur got out of the car and opened the rear door and stepped aside holding the handle.

Groany rising, the commandant stood on the pavement and ignored the chauffeur and foot stomped and arched and pinched his hip and watched the doorway. 'My suitcase, Jan.'

The chauffeur shut the door and opened the boot and leaned over four jerry tanks and lifted two suitcases, the smaller one his own. He hurried ahead and put the suitcases on the steps and held the glass doors open. The commandant strode past him, yellow alight, into the lobby.

Candelabrum lamps burned on velvet red walls. Dim teardrop bulbs. The carpet a red wall match. A snug lobby. Low ceiling, expanding into a lounge, tables and chairs, cutlery and napkins set. End corner a bar reception. A man stood there, his back to the lobby. He faced the gantry, slim and silent, white shirtsleeves, black waistcoat, arms folded, smoke rising from his tilt head. A mouth stuck cigarette. Admiring his shoes, the commandant thought.

The commandant waved his chauffeur to wait near the doors. He cut past tables and chairs and noisy breathed at the bar and watched the man and the smoke. In the mirror gantry the commandant saw the man's nose and brow and ears grin-lift.

'Courvoisier,' the commandant Polish said, seeing the cognac among fat bottle liquors and vermouths and spirits rigged on the gantry wood. 'I am right for that.'

Smoke wove from the man.

'I am right for it.' He ratted the bartop with a signet ring pinkie. 'Ready as a cobbler, you.'

Smoking, the man stared at the floor.

The commandant pointed at a wall. 'I see electricity here. A lucky hotel. Same as one I know. I said it to Jan Domarski. He is my secretary over there.' He looked at the doors and didn't see his chauffeur. Suitcases too gone.

He turned to the man's hair and smoke and said, 'I missed the bellboy.'

The man stayed dummy, his smoke roofward, curling thicker.

'I would guess this hotel and the hotel I know are from the same blueprint.' The commandant short laughed. 'It is a common thing.'

The man freeze stood there.

'I am Kazimiers Kapka. Architect,' he jumpy said. 'I know about this. It is usual to make many hotels from one blueprint. Hear me, you? What is the matter? Are you deaf or daft? I want a room. Damn it, I want that bottle.'

A hiss came from the bar. The commandant thought it a pressure fault of a keg. Then the man's shoulders lifted and sunk and veins piped his neck and smoke rose blacker and the commandant traced the hiss to the smokerise. He backward stepped from the bar and shouted, 'Bellboy, bellboy, bellboy,' and his hind bumped a chair and he sat and slapped the table and said, 'Bellboy, you.'

Muddle thinking, he watched the hair and heard the hiss and saw the man billow.

From a hall off the lobby a lady entered the lounge.

The commandant turned away from the man and watched the lady and better breathed. She moved snakeslither. Sat at a table under a wall space. He stared at her. Relished her display. Her hair fall. Her mouth swell. Her fur coat woman shape. She lifted the napkin and small folded it and put it on her cheek and headbow started to cry.

Snap planning to mind her, the commandant tugged his tie knot and stood up.

A stout dickie-tuxedo man came from the hall and went to her table and whispered to her face. She dropped the napkin and followed him out of the lounge.

Crashing past chairs, the commandant shouted, 'Wait there. Oy, you, wait you.'

Hallway, the light weakened. Lamps flicker buzzed. The commandant quick marched and the hall corner-turned. A short march and another turn. A left and a right and another left. A maze way. Round a turn, a boy wearing a blue ornate uniform waited lobby-end in an open elevator. He said, 'Going up,' and the commandant wild marched up the carpet.

'Where did he take her? Fatso. What room?'

'Third floor for you, sir,' the boy said, and he turned a dial to three.

'God, if he knew me. I swear, you. If he knew me.'

The elevator surged upward, a wall-grate moan.

'Pig. He will see. I am Herr Commandant.' He creasenose nodded and smirk said, 'Our secret, ha, you.'

A bell rang. The elevator halted and the boy yanked open the grill. 'Third floor, sir.' The commandant stepped out and turned to address the boy. The elevator had gone clanky downfloor, the grill shut.

'Our secret, you,' he shouted downshaft. 'Between us.'

The floor was neat and long and red. Doors ribbed the walls. The commandant couldn't see the carpet's end. Up the hall the line thinned and shrunk and walls illusion met in a thick dark.

He went wall-to-wall, halting and listening, door to door alert uphall.

Door 109 was warm. Sticky heat. Ear against the panel he heard a male voice. He couldn't make the words. He heard thumping. Repetitive hits. Like a rug getting beat. Firmer pressing the door he heard crying and thuds and talk. He knocked, a fist salvo, and shouted, 'You, what is it in there?'

Noises came bolder.

'Is it her?'

Louder rose the din.

'Oy, mister. A party, ha.'

Looser the noise.

'Is she yours, you?' Game buoyant, he tried the handle and the door opened and the smell caught him.

Human salts. Semen and urine and glands. Male and female fluids dilute. Smacks of tobacco and beer and breath. The walls were flamelit. Mantled with shadows. Candles on a corner table. Four poster bed, draped with black gauze and silk. Like a grand hearse.

Bedside, a robed man sat. Frail aged. Robe open. Penis on his thigh, bloat and pale and leaking. He mouthgape watched the sobbing woman on the bed. Erect on her hands and knees. Tarred and feathered. Head shaven. Pores weeping steam.

A nude man covered her. Crust old as the bedside man. Madder mouthgaped. Suckered on her. A man mollusc. He gripped her chin and pulled and craned her neck. His eyes bubbled. He groaned and jerked and spat and drawl sang, 'Rhine drinker drink it, drink it up,' rowing with her. The mattress thumped. Bone fingers raked her spine. 'Rhine drinker drink it, drink it up, drink drink drink, drink your muck.'

Ulcers bled and feathers puffed and float and fell and he rowed on singsong.

Bottom of the bed the dickie-tuxedo man sat on a chair smoking a cigar. The woman faced him. He tasted his cigar and blew. 'Glorious,' he said, sweat shiny, watching her move melodic in the smoke shroud. Keeping her watch, he said, 'Hello, Alois.'

'Ha. You mistake me for someone.' The commandant held the door and entered a step. 'I am Kazimiers Kapka.'

Dickie-tuxedo belched smoke at the woman. 'See her. Corrine Dusang.'

'I do not know the name.'

'You turned her.'

'Ha. I am not the man.'

'Infested her.'

'Your head is sick. I think so.'

'Vichy. March 23rd 1942. Alois Seeler met Corinne Dusang. A sunny day.'

'See a nut quack, you.'

'Springtime Vichy. Herr Commandant on leave.'

'I am Kazimiers Kapka.'

'Hotel Hermitage. The viper den. You owned her there.'

'Are you deaf or daft?'

Dickie-tuxedo crushed his cigar on a bedpost and dropped the smoulder stub on a feather pile. Through the smoke he fondled the woman's cheek. 'Cherish his endurance.' He winked at the crooner oldster and strolled to a wall and touched the mating shadow and stared at the commandant. 'She was your flower.'

'Deaf and daft, you.'

'Madam Petals,' he bawled.

Candleflames waved like flags. The shadow burst and drip-spelled COLLABORATOR wall-splat huge and black. Then the shadow played again into the mating form and the woman's cry and the song came from the bed and the wall.

'Funny tricks, ha.'

'Our tulip now.' Dickie-tuxedo's eyes brainturned and his crotch lumped and his face jiggled and clicked and his jaw collapsed chestrest and he shirtspit climbed onto the bed and the bedside man boarded the bed and the three sires dragged and mounted the featherfly woman and rattle sang, 'Rhine drinker drink it, drink it up.'

Brave empty, the commandant ducked out of the room and ran along the hall, a breathy shambles. From a gap the boy stepped out and said, 'Going down, sir.'

He barged into the elevator. 'Hurry, you, hurry.'

Grill shut, the boy cranked the dial and the box went moany down.

'My suitcase.' The commandant slackened his tie and opened his collar and sweatdrip said, 'My luger is there.'

The boy watched the dial.

'Hear me, you.'

A bell rang. The commandant pushed the boy and pulled the grill and rushed out and his motion carried him into darkness.

'Underfloor,' the boy said, and slammed the elevator shut.

Bulblight shot upshaft.

'Ha. Big laughs,' the commandant shouted, and arm hacked the blackness. 'If you knew me, you.'

Air blasted and the ground vibrated. Sounded like a blowtorch igniting. In smother darkness a window glowed. Orange lit a chamber. 'Oy, you.' He finger wagged at the light, his sight coming. 'Stay there, you.'

Quick marching, he saw the vault. A rusted gurney sat near the iron door. He looked through the orange window.

Fire devoured his chauffeur. He jived. Jumped freakshow. Clown kicker legs. His arms bizarre chopping. He stiffened and his hands switched ticktock. Like he was warding traffic. Frenzy ablaze, he ticktocked and headnod and peeled, his face gaped, a skullmelt bawl.

'Funny tricks,' the commandant said, cold riddled, clarity feeling the living he done and the living he could have did.

On the window his face mirrored. His time showed on the glaze. Cot to now. A life spate. He saw him infant precious. Saw him son worthy. Saw him brownshirted. Saw him Sieg heil blackclad.

He saw yesterday. The sedan upturned in a ditch. Chauffeur and him rigor ruined.

Final he saw him warrant mothers and fathers and children to smoke. Murder vapour, adrift silver. Soul shoals ethered.

He undressed and lay on the gurney. Bare as him born. From a colder dark his chauffeur foot-drag shuffled to him. Ember skin chunks. Bones charred. A cinder man. He pushed the gurney squeak-wheel and ash fell and trailed and he crackle said, 'When you are done you heal. Then you go in again.'

The iron door opened and the commandant lifted and tilted and slid to his price end.

Last purity he saw was the Serbian girl's hair. Spilled from his ditchside wallet. A gust took it. Ran the tied fringe along the road. It rolled and rose windlift and circled up past the firtops and sailed away.

THE SENSE OF AN ENDING

TIM SYKES

The End 'The Sense of an Ending' (2015)
Gloss and masonry paint on canvas
51 x 66cm

THE END: FIFTEEN ENDINGS TO FIFTEEN PAINTINGS

The thing came to pass toward nightfall, confirming the presentiments he had suffered all afternoon. It was bisected by a deep fissure, like a cloven sky. Points of light glinted on its viscous surface.

Vanya placed the callipers and ruler on the tiles. A pencil lay ready in the gutter of the journal. He removed the rubber gloves. He wrote:

26 April 1997 21:40
187 x 48mm;
Consistency – firm (moderate stickiness);
Odour – sweet-foul;
Hue – exceptionally dark;
Supplementary remarks: –

He closed the journal. He reopened it and struck through the last five words. The lightbulb cast a yellow glow on the shower curtain, similar to the glow of a sun setting beneath storm clouds.

… Hue – black;
Supplementary remarks: Vile creature. Doubts fade.

He went to his bedroom and sat in wait for the next one.

Next morning two or three-dozen comrades had gathered to buttress the Revolution – better than the previous Sunday. Patches of dirty snow lingered. When would spring finally arrive?

'… the unbendable rails of the steam locomotive of History, comrades, head directly towards the terminus of Communism,' said the orator. 'Let the drunkard of the Counter-Revolution stagger onto the tracks of historical materialism. Comrades! Shall he derail the locomotive? Can you not perceive the terminus?'

There were murmurs. Vanya nodded.

At a certain distance, occupying the centre of the square, were the anarchists, both of them dressed in black and hopping about in the cold. Over to the left, in front of the Winter Palace, a curly-haired boy was peddling anti-Semitic newspapers. He gave Vanya a wave.

The meeting concluded.

A grizzled man emerged from the crowd, removing his glove to shake hands.

'Ivan,' he said, 'how are you living? Are you acquainted with Comrade Grushova?'

'Very bad, Mikhailich,' said Vanya. 'Worse.'

'Young blood!' smiled Comrade Grushova. She extended her sharp nails.

Vanya regarded Comrade Grushova. She was made up like a tigress.

'Please, call me Natasha. I'm not so very many years your senior, am I? You'll be here on the holiday? – The Party expects you.'

'Health permitting.'

'A vigorous young man? It's vital we swell the ranks.'

The revolutionaries were beginning to disperse, warning each other. 'Better watch the ice with that hip of yours, Gennady Sergeyevich.'

A gunmetal sky hung over Palace Square.

That evening's had been more troubling: soft and coloured like a pale horse, a crimson spot glaring at one end.
Vanya dug his knuckles into his belly. He took the fountain pen and began copying from the journal into the logbook.

27 April 1997 19:05
156 x 45mm;
Consistency – soft;

Odour – odourless;
Hue – cream. Marked with evil eye.
Supplementary remarks: beetroot not consumed in over 48 hours.

He waited for the ink to dry, his eyes twinkling in the half-light, before reviewing the entries in the logbook from the beginning. Following the latest entry there remained just three unfilled pages, after which came a series of appendices containing tables, charts and illustrations. There was a line graph on the final page. Its axes were unlabelled. A violent arc slashed the upper third of the page. The line of the graph kept always below this rough, black curve, though the trend suggested it was only a matter of time before they intersected. Vanya made a dot just below the slash, diverting the trend upward.

He put the logbook aside and resumed marking his witless students' geometry exams.

The sad photograph of his father gazed from the wall.

The doctor pulled out of his pocket a pack of White Sea Canal cigarettes. Vanya declined.

'Blood? That's what they all say. It wasn't blood, I tell them, but probably a bit of beetroot.' The doctor lit a cigarette.

'Not only the crimson spot,' said Vanya. 'Other signs. A marked escalation.' He dropped the logbook on the table.

'I don't know a soul who doesn't enjoy a plate of borsch.'

'Are no further procedures ...? ... given consideration of my family history ...'

The doctor strolled to the window. Smoke rolled over his shoulders.

'Akh ... what can you do in a land where nothing happens? Come back in twenty years and sit on this windowsill, those wretched kiosks will still be rusting on the corner, selling the same spirits, dill and mounds of potatoes. Stagnation! Last week I went to buy apples – my wife asked for apples – and the kiosk aunty says, "Don't take a fancy to those, unless you've a stables to feed. They're autumn apples – finished."'

'Apple disagrees with me in general,' said Vanya. 'As for beetroot …'

'You've seen the fruits in Prisma? Works of art! Perfection! My wife and I visit the Finnish supermarket as we visit the State Hermitage Museum. But Russia will never be like a Finnish supermarket.' The doctor opened the window and tossed his smouldering filter into the wind. 'Russia's a still life of rotting apples in a rusted kiosk.'

'That's mistaken,' said Vanya. 'History progresses toward a crisis. Its fabric stretches and is doomed to tear. Things must fall apart.'

'If you insist, Ivan … As for your condition – incurable.'

The logbook lay on the kitchen table. Vanya's fingers trembled.

1 May 1997 06:57

It moved!

Was watching it closely. A distinct pulse.

Mutable, dimensions indistinct.

Texture was pitted. Like a poison toad.

Yes. Moving. Breathing. There are more inside me.

He opened the freezer and took them all out. Each of the transparent bags bore a tag. He sorted them chronologically. Then, consulting the last page of the logbook, he arranged them on the kitchen table to reproduce the line of the graph. He examined them again to verify the values, cackling 'yes! indeed! ha! ha! yes!' Then he took the fresh bag and he saw there was no space for it on the table. And he marked a final dot on the graph, so that the line at last crossed the awful slash in the page. Sweat shimmered on his face. Across the inside back cover he wrote:

THE END

He closed the logbook, got up and dashed out of the front door.

The pavement was crammed. A procession of trade unionists, the robbed and the humiliated made its way up Nevsky Prospekt. Solitary snowflakes frolicked in the air. Vanya panted, hastening through the throng, squeezed and elbowed. As the marchers reached the square the protest diffused into the general May Day festivity. There was dancing under red banners. A wrinkled dwarf was playing the accordion. Around her they were singing about the future:

>We build the road to joyfulness –
>
>Upon it march forth to Stalin!

Mikhailich stumbled forward, quite drunk, pulling off his glove.

'Vanechka my dear boy! What a day! A little foretaste of the merriness at the end of history, eh?'

Someone crept up behind Vanya and covered his eyes with the palms of her hands.

'Guess who!'

'Oh, Comrade Grushova, it's you ... The lines, they intersected ...'

'But you're pale! You've a fever. Natashenka must take care of you.'

She fondled Vanya's hair.

Mikhailich reeled into the multitude and vanished.

Comrade Grushova pursed her lips. She took Vanya's hand.

'Come, this is no place for a poorly child.'

Over Comrade Grushova's bed was a poster that depicted a black panther reposing upon a white piano. On the table stood a framed photograph of her late husband in military uniform. She took the cup from Vanya.

'There, there, my frogling. Are you now at ease?'

'I feel more comfortable,' said Vanya. 'You have been kind, Natasha.'

'You see, it was your nerves. You're not gravely ill. Just your nerves are frayed.'

A tear welled in her eyeshadow.

'I was moved, Vanya, when I saw how you were.'
She stroked his brow ... and his face, neck, chest.
Vanya shut his eyes. His head swam.
Matters progress towards crises. The fabric tears.

He caught Comrade Grushova's wrist and pulled her onto the bed. She gasped and then sighed and continued to caress him.

It began to twinge in his belly. An infinite line is eventually cut.

He could sense it now, yes, in the dark: the ending – yes! – creeping closer ...

Comrade Grushova mewled.

ALL THE TVs IN TOWN

DAN POWELL

The End 'All the TVs in Town' (2015)
Gloss and masonry paint on canvas
51 x 66cm

It was the writing that stopped her, made her peer closely at the station sign and strain to read what was scribbled there. Behind her she could feel the sun as it fell below the rooftops of the buildings that lined the opposite platform. The last of the day's warmth slipped like fingers across the back of her neck for a moment before the cooler air of the evening brushed them away. Jon was halfway down the platform before he realised she had stopped. He dropped their hold-all to the ground before turning back to watch her lean in to read what was written there.

On the main portion of the sign, in bold white on black, the name of the station was clearly visible.

Shoeburyness.

In the cherry red square to the left of the name, in thin black marker, in a spidery hand, someone had scrawled a definition.

– that uncomfortable feeling one experiences when sitting in a chair that is still warm from the last occupant.

She traced a finger along some of the letters, followed the jag and swish of ascenders and descenders to their abrupt ends. The precise, clipped lettering of the word 'Shoeburyness' on the main portion of the sign, its font selected by some executive deep in the corporate web of c2c, made the writing in the cherry square to the left appear all the more esoteric.

It's Douglas Adams, Jon said.

He was beside her, and peered in close to read the writing himself. Behind them the train stood empty, its internal carriage lights flickering against the growing dark.

It's from The Meaning of Liff.

Liff?

L.i.f.f. It's a dictionary he made up with someone else, full of things there aren't words for yet.

Weren't words for then, you mean?

What?

When was it written?

She stopped tracing the crooked, jagged letters and turned to face Jon, watched him stare off to the left, his eyes searching of the space around him, the outward action mirroring his internal rummaging through memory.

The 1980's I suppose. Somewhere then.

So presumably there are words for those things now, because he wrote them.

Jon hauled up the holdall, swung it to his shoulder.

Can we get going? he said.

The sun had vanished behind the rooftops surrounding the station, leaving behind a deep red streak in the west. The station seemed to shrink as the dark weight of night began to press down upon the sparse lighting that dotted the platform. The sound of their footsteps upon the concrete and tarmac was almost smothered by a bass hum that growled from the electrical installations caged behind railings at the station boundary.

She scanned the station for some sign of a ticket inspector or station staff or any other passengers. At the terminus of the line her gaze was drawn to the buffers. The blunt heavy discs pressed out from the shadows, seemed to float above the rails like two improbable full stops that marked the abrupt end of the line's reach and its vanishing point.

Was there no one else with us on the train? she said.

No idea, Jon called back over his shoulder.

The exit was open and deserted. Only the little green arrows and red crosses illuminated on the sides of the barriers indicated how to enter, how to exit. Jon stepped through a gate marked with a red cross. She stepped to the side, passed through a gate marked with a green arrow and followed him off the platform.

You shouldn't do that, she called after him.

Jon, perhaps not hearing, said nothing.

In the station entrance the departure and arrival screens displayed no listings. Instead a grainy grey image flickered from every display; a black circle inset with a grey triangle itself inset with the initials **CD**, and emblazoned across this logo, in sketchily shaded block capitals, two words:

THE END.

That's weird. They spoke the words at the same time, caught themselves and smiled.

Across the bottom of the image in smaller block capitals:

TELEVISION RIGHTS RESERVED.

Must be some sort of screensaver, come on, Jon said. He hefted their holdall to his shoulder and stepped out into the street.

She looked over to the ticket office. The glass doors were closed, the space behind thick with shadow that revealed just the hint of empty chairs beyond the grey outline of desks and closed down computers.

Isn't it still a bit early for them to be closed up? Ours wasn't the last train, was it?

She meant her questions for Jon but already he was too far along the road ahead to hear.

The streets outside were as quiet as the station. Parked cars lined the kerbs but nothing moved along the patched and potholed tarmac of the road. Away down the high street the pale red glow of temporary traffic signals illuminated a line of cones, the road there empty where vehicles should have growled and shuddered, impatient for the light to change. The thin light of the street lamps shivered in the air about them, trembling as if from the cool of the evening.

They walked abreast of each other for a while without speaking, holding hands tightly. His pulse tripped through the ends of his fingers to hers, and she felt it beat and counter-beat with her own. The sensation distracted her from the once familiar streets surrounding them, filled her conscious thought, became a kind of communication, a call and response, each pulse urging forth the next beat from the other. Until Jon, needing to heft the bag to his other shoulder, let her hand slip from his.

The straps are biting my hand, he said.

He wriggled the fingers and thumb of his right hand and she glimpsed bright red and pale white bands pressed into his skin, where the weight of the bag had stopped the blood in places, trapped it in pools in others. They moved on again without speaking until, a few streets deeper into town, she stopped on the pavement, her head cocked, listening for the electrical hum that seemed to have followed them from the platform. It hung in the air, under the sound of Jon's footsteps as he continued up the street ahead of her.

Do you hear that?

What?

There's a hum.

A hum?

In the air somewhere.

He did not move back to her but stood where he had stopped. She held her breath. They stared at each other over cracked paving slabs spotted with grey spots of old gum. They both listened.

I don't hear anything, he said finally.

Seriously? You don't hear that?

No. I don't hear anything. I don't hear any traffic, any noises from the houses here. He paused and they both looked around at the pallid glow of the windows of the houses lining the street. There's no doors banging, no dogs barking, no babies crying, no voices but ours.

She realised he was right. Her attention had been so drawn

by the hum suspended under the sound of their footsteps, the hiss and puff of her own breathing, that she had not noticed the absence of other ambient sound. There seemed to be no lights on in the houses along the street, except in what she thought must be the living room of each one, and even there only a flickering blue light escaped, the zombie glow of a horde of flat screen TVs.

It's like we're the only ones here. He laughed as he said this, a clipped wry sounding chuckle at the ridiculousness of the idea, then hefted the holdall again and spun on his heels. Let's get a shift on. I'm dying for the loo.

She still had a key for her parents' house, the house she grew up in, and she let them both in. Here too, all lights were off, and the same ashen blue glow of the TV, flickered from the half open living room door.

Hello? We're here, she called, her voice sounding thin and childlike as it echoed back to her. She stepped into the thin hall of the terrace and Jon followed, dumping the holdall under a row of hooks smothered with a multitude of coats, most of them child-size.

That's my coat from primary school.

She lifted a small brown duffel coat with tapered wooden buttons. A pair of green woollen mittens, fixed with cord to the coat, dangled, one from each sleeve cuff.

Mum knitted those. Said I could pick the wool from the shop down the high street.

She slipped the forefingers of her right hand into a mitten, the wool stretching, then pulled the coat to her face and breathed in the smell of it.

God, it smells of my old school. Chalk dust, Marmite sandwiches, old wood.

As touching as this is, which way is the loo?

She lowered the coat, looked to where Jon was jigging from foot to foot. The bulk of him made the movement ridiculous.

Straight up, the door at the top.

As he tramped upstairs she rehung the coat on its hook, trailed her fingers through the others; her fur-lined parka from secondary school, bright blue, the one mum always called her tomboy coat; the trench coat she wore all through college and university, hanging along with the jet black scarf Mum had knitted her; the tie-died denim jacket that she wore to her first ever Glastonbury.

I can't believe Mum kept these.

What?

Jon's raised voice shoved past the still closed door of the bathroom, barrelled down the stairs to her.

Nothing. Just the coats. I can't believe she kept them. That she has them hanging up.

She stood at the bottom of the stairs, head cocked to listen for his reply. When none came, she slipped into the kitchen. Unwashed dinner plates smeared with gravy sat ready beside a full bowl of washing up water, the fresh white bubbles brimming up above the lip of the bowl. Without thinking she dipped a couple of fingers of her hand into the water. Hot. She shook the foam from her fingers crossed to the kettle, where two mugs stood, a fresh tea bag in each waiting for water. A thin trail of steam slipped from the spout of the kettle. Hesitantly she pressed the tips of her fingers to the side of the kettle, jerked them back before the hot metal surface could burn her skin. On the kitchen table, her parents' placemats and water glasses remained, laid at their usual seats, the salt and pepper shakers left where they had been placed during the meal, not returned to the condiment tray as her mother always insisted.

She made her way back down the hall and called back up the stairs to Jon.

You OK up there, you haven't fallen down the u-bend have you?

Nearly finished. A small grunt like he made when he was lifting something heavy strained out between the words.

You're not having a shit up there are you?

A pause strained out for a moment. Two.
Perhaps.
Just make sure you flush it properly. And open a window.
Yes, Mum.
His tone was jovial, only a little teasing, a little sarcastic, but she flinched at it as she would a blow.

In the living room the curtains were closed to the growing night outside and the lights and lamps were off. In the corner of the room, between the bay window and the fireplace, a hulking, new flat-screen loomed atop the battered wooden TV cupboard she remembered from her childhood. The light from the screen threw shadows across the room, made shapes in the empty armchair and sofa seats, little pools of darkness where her mother and father would usually be sat at this time, watching *Gardeners' World* or some travel documentary. On the screen the same grainy grey image from the train station displays flickered, the black circle set in a grey triangle itself inset with the initials CD. The two words in block capitals and rendered in scratched grey shading to appear three dimensional, seemed now to push out of the screen towards her.

THE END.

A syrupy weariness poured through her and she dropped into her father's armchair, stretched back, let her head fall back to the cushioned rest behind, closed her eyes. The warmth of the seat, thick and present, moved through the thin denim of her jeans, the cotton of her tee, reached her skin as the smell of her father, earth and sun and cigarettes, still hanging in the air about the chair, filled her nostrils.

Shoeburyness.

Except the warmth grew, heating her, as if another body was still present in the chair with her. She placed a hand on the armrest, and the heat of the chair amplified in that way heat does when two bodies are held together. She half-imagined a hand, her father's hand, broad and rough skinned from years of work, placed down upon hers. She almost convinced herself that it was there, did not wish to move, but the heat of the chair grew uncomfortable and she pulled herself up. She slipped to the sofa, made at first for her usual seat at the opposite end to where her mother always sat, then stopped herself and slumped down on her mother's seat instead. This too was warm and the air around it heavy with the smell of laundry detergent, boiled veg and thin Avon perfume. She managed longer this time, let the warmth in the seat grow once more until her discomfort forced her to her feet. For no reason she could wrangle into words, she sat once more only this time selected the seat of the sofa that had always hung empty between herself and her mother. She kicked off her shoes, pulled her legs up, put her knees to her chin, her feet flat on the seat cushion, wrapped her arms around her shins. The warmth in this seat was just her own and she gazed out over the mountain peak of her kneecaps at the screen. The image and words seemed entirely the same as the one they had seen, she and Jon, in the train station, seemed the same even as she had seen it when she first entered the living room, but now, she read the words running across the bottom of the screen as **TELEVISION RIGHTS REVERSED.** She rubbed her eyes, squinted, read the words again.

The sound of the toilet flushing upstairs pulled her from the sofa and back out into the hall. She turned and looked up the stairs, listened for the click in the lock of the bathroom door that would herald Jon's emergence from the bathroom. She stared at the door, but the door did not open. She held herself still, listened for the sound of a tap running or his booted feet on the floor above but heard neither. The hum, the jagged electrical bass that had followed them through the streets from the station was the only sound beyond those she made herself.

You coming down?

The sound of her own voice surprised her. She heard shades of her mother and father in the accent and tone, thicker now she was home again, despite her not having heard a voice other than her own and Jon's since a stop or two prior to their arrival. Jon laughed whenever she answered the phone to her parents, at how her voice changed when she spoke to them.

That weird screen is on the TVs here too. It's starting to creep me out.

She climbed the stairs slowly, listened between the soft creaks squeezed from each step for some sound beyond the hum that seemed, though its volume did not grow, to have swollen with further frequencies the bulk of the sound fattening and spreading. She heard nothing more than the sound of herself.

The bathroom door was closed and she rapped on it with a raised knuckle.

Jon, you still in there? You OK?

She waited for a moment, sure that he was about to throw open the door and step out. When he did not she tried the handle. The door, unlocked, opened easily.

I'm coming in. I don't want to see your hairy arse so pull your pants up, she called through, then waited a moment before stepping inside.

The bathroom was empty and silent but for the hum and a thin trickling sound that itself trickled across the top of the fuzzing sound. She crossed to the sink. A thin line of water trailed from the cold tap, and the plug hole gurgled at it greedily. The taps were old, the same ones she remembered from childhood, and as she slipped her hand over the four spoked handle, felt the bulbous metal tears of the spoke ends, their curves pressing to the skin of her palm, she felt for that moment like a child again.

Jon, if this is you mucking about, I'm not in the mood.

She stepped onto the landing, listened for an answer, or for some telltale sign of where he was hiding. In her parents' room the lights were off and the curtains open. A broad full moon hung in the sky to the rear of the house and threw light enough for her to see that there was no one, not her parents, not Jon, in there. She grabbed her phone from the pocket of her jeans, tapped the unlock button but the screen remained dark for a moment. Two. She expected the empty battery symbol to appear, not the grainy image from the train station, from the TV.

THE END.

She ran down the stairs, threw the front door open, burst out into the street. The street lamps were out and as far along the pavement as she could see, the only light, apart from the grey-blue glow that fuzzed against the living room windows of every house on the street, was the high definition glow of the too-broad moon which hung too low and too large and seemed to tremble in the too black sky that pressed down upon the rooftops. A few doors along she noticed a living room window that glowed somewhat brighter than the others and she ran to it. The ashen glow of the TV washed over another deserted sofa. On the screen: **THE END.** She looked up and down the street, saw the same grey-blue light escaping from cracks in curtains, slipping through sallow net curtains, bursting from those few houses with open curtains or no curtains at all. She remembered the train station, half the town away.

Back inside her house, she tried the remote first, jabbing buttons, stabbing the it at the screen before her. The TV refused to acknowledge the invisible infrared commands that fired from the remote, refused to change channel, refused to turn off, even when she used the buttons on the TV itself.

Jon? Dad? Mum?

She shouted the words at first. Again. The fear in her voice made her jump and she hurled the remote at the screen. She expected it to shatter the surface, fracture the image, spill the colours lurking in the pixels, send them swirling in an oil slick rainbow across the dead grey of **THE END**. The impact did not even scuff the surface and the remote thumped quietly into the carpet.

She stepped back without taking her eyes from the screen, dropped into her own seat on the sofa, her usual seat, pulled her feet up behind her. As a child she'd played that game children play, where the floor is lava and the only way around the room is to walk on the furniture. How her mother had screamed when she'd played that game. She wished to hear even that sound now, instead of the hum that fuzzed thick and wide beneath everything. She raised her knees again, placed her chin on the peak of them, and stared into the bluegrey glow of the screen. The hum, that still roar, that howled whisper, that had followed her from the station broadened further now, become almost a cloud of voices, too hushed and intermingled to distinguish. She thought for a moment that she should be looking for someone but her thoughts failed to fix on exactly who and the image dragged her back.

THE END.

The thick black shading of the letters no longer seemed to press the words out from the screen. Instead, each block capital seemed to be falling into the scrawl of the grey background. As her eyes followed the trailing of each letter into a black chute of its own shape, she noticed the seat beneath her was warm.

NOWHERE NOTHING FUCK-UP
UV RAY

The End 'Nowhere Nothing Fuck-Up' (2015)
Gloss and masonry paint on canvas
51 x 66cm

THE END: FIFTEEN ENDINGS TO FIFTEEN PAINTINGS

working the night shift in the cubicle farm days fold into days and nights fold into nights losing all cohesion   we're packed in like battery hens and all you know is you've got to start making plans to get away   the cubes are three feet square and you can see over the top of the prefabricated partitions and right next to me i've got this guy called len zelock who happily taps away at his computer like the only one in the place whose brain hasn't been turned to mush by this job because it was already fucking mush before he started and i can see the top of his bald head bobbing about as he enters updates into his spreadsheet and he sings this song going   der are zo menee pussy faahmers   der are zo menee pussy faahmers   except for the fact i think he's german or something and he pronounces pussy as puzzy   he sings that one tedious line from the song over and over and over again day in day out and i don't know what the fucking song is but he sings it non stop until you end up wanting to banjo him i've got a paper cup of lifeless vending machine coca cola on my desk in front of me   in fact it's not actually coca cola at all it's flat and tastes like cough tincture and i only get it so i can surreptitiously stir in some amphetamine to keep me going and when i got up out of my chair to go to the machine i asked len zelock if he wanted anything and without shifting his eyes from his monitor he said fedge me a packet of dry roasted and i go okay sure and he adds   dry roasted don't fedge me no pistachios they're for homo zexuals all of us here are half way to the point of total annihilation and the world around us is just a globular pulp you can feel the walls closing in you don't feel anything really hopes and dreams all paralysed i never lived through the normal channels other people live through a reject from birth what more could i do but disconnect from the world? the tiny travel alarm clock i keep on my desk goes tick tock tick tock tick tock

in the placidity of cool blue morning after my shift the orange streetlights start switching themselves off i spot a forty year old ford cortina up a side street near the sunset cinema club that's a piece of piss to steal and it took me a few seconds to wangle the door barrel with the screwdriver i carry about with me i took off my jacket and placed it folded on the passenger seat before bombing my last gram of crank hot wiring the ignition and driving the shitbox away rolling down the window i sit well back in the driver's seat spark up a smoke and crack open the bottle of beer i got in my jacket pocket and drive holding the bottle between my legs with the cool dawn breeze blowing on my face driving driving driving petrol stations and pylons city lights like camera flashes in my dilated eyes i flick on the radio and lynard skynyrd's freebird is playing so i turn up the juice as high as it will go and smoke my cigarette with my arm resting on the door inside my head i'm thinking back to my word association test …

glass?

opaque

truth?

fragile

message?

oblique

speech?

lies

child?

scar

no i said i didn't think it possible for people to change   love and hate tattooed across the knuckles of your hands   there was no such thing as metamorphosis in a human being whether through god or the devil or baptism or death or reincarnation or anything else   except maybe unless ... like let's say someone murdered you and fed you to the dogs on the street and afterwards the dogs shitted you out and all that was left of you was a stinking pile of dogshit   that would be a metamorphosis of a sorts don't you think?   dr weiss's impartial facade slipped briefly and for a second he kind of looked at me funny   he scrawled something down on his pad silver pen glinting in the table light and pushed his glasses back up on his nose and said   i suppose that's one way of looking at it   the doctor crossed his bony legs and added perhaps we'll explore that thought in greater depth during your next session

driving   driving   driving barrelling the car full pelt needle touching ninety and it feels like kerosene pumping through my veins thinking about broken dreams and broken loves and broken everyfuckingthings thinking about what if the love you buy is perhaps the only kind of real love there is?   i've become just this cold and numb human being this figment watching the rest of the world from the outside through a soundproof unbreakable pane of glass that separates me from them and them from me and i bang on the glass but no one hears and no one looks my way like i don't exist at all   no one knows of this dead heart corroding in my chest like a ship at the bottom of an ocean where fish turn and twist   turn and twist   like silver coins glittering in its iron carcass of drowned souls   i cannot recall the last time i felt a real emotion or at any time anyone else's life ever touching mine but if the past exists only in our minds as fractured memories then i've come to the conclusion that the same must also be true of the present and therefore nothing matters anyway nothing is real   maybe life is just a series of events between cigarettes and television shows and it's all just a question of how long it takes life to shatter your delusions   and sooner or later it always does   life will break you in the end   it breaks everyone in the end

i pulled in a 24-7 supermarket and bought vodka and cigarettes   i drove onwards without any direction in mind i drove the motorway until the stars diminished and the sky turned an explosive shade of early morning yellow streaked with fiery red airplane vapour trails and the sun looked like a dull flat red disc simmering low on the horizon   i drove until the old ford ran out of fuel and abandoned it where it stalled to a halt by the side of the road in the middle of a derelict industrial estate   i'd ended up on the outskirts of some cold northern town somewhere that looked like a seamless sheet of bleak battleship grey   it'd be like 8 am or something by now and i pulled my leather jacket on and zipped it up   i jumped out the car and started walking   tall nettles sprouted up through cracks in the disused pavements and the wind whistled through the empty dead shells of factories inside one of which i found a small room that looked like it once would have been an office or storeroom of some sort where the only indication of life was an old mattress on the concrete floor in the corner and beside it a discarded old dog-eared porno magazine   empty beer cans and cigarette stubs scattered about the floor

i set my carrier bag of booze and cigarettes down next to me on the floor and lay back on the mattress with my back propped up against the wall   i spark up another smoke and grab the porno and flick through the stiffened pages   confronted with a double page close up of a vagina i realise the very notion of the whole trauma of birth fills me with repulsion   it's all a matter of hospitals and blood and doctors and screaming agony   it will be much better in the future when we are created in laboratories and raised in glass domes fed by tubes until our brains and muscles and limbs are all properly formed totally remove the human aspect of it altogether   if i could choose i'd choose not to be human at all i'd choose to be born a flower growing in complete isolation up a remote mountain somewhere unseen and untouched by the rest of humanity

i can no longer find any beauty in the world   i no longer even believe in beauty   when i look at a tree i see a tree everything in black and white   and the sea is just the sea and the stars just the stars nothing more than that   life is just one immense clockwork machine and if your blood flows different to theirs they'll take you and rip the veins out your flesh   you can walk down the street like any man can walk down the street but you're the man without a face for the world to see   all there is finally is the inevitability of human decay and one day you'll be gone from the world with no more input into it and no more knowledge of it and without you the merry go round will just keep turning its eternal revolutions forever   everything eventually fades away and between then and now time passes like a slow scalpel through your flesh draining you of blood rendering you ever weaker and weaker until everything and everyone loses the fight in the end and falls into the abyss the eternal terror of nothingness   a terrifying discarnate voice that says   i don't know who i am   and you can feel yourself fading away disappearing from view   the dead may well stay alive in a way in the minds of those that knew them but they too will eventually fade away   everything is transitory and in the end we all succumb to the final meaningless ultimatum of our own personal armageddon

i twist off the cap on the smirnoff bottle and take a long draw on my cigarette and gaze upwards to exhale the hot blue smoke from my lungs and take a swig of the vodka   graffiti sprayed in big black letters across the damp grey ceiling says all hail death! we will storm the gates together!

AUTHORS

AJ Ashworth's collection Somewhere Else, or Even Here won the Scott Prize and was shortlisted in the Edge Hill Prize. She also edited *Red Room: New Short Stories Inspired by the Brontes* (Unthank Books). www.ajashworth.com

Gordon Collins has been a market risk analyst, a maths lecturer, an English teacher in Japan and a computer graphics researcher specialising in virtual humans. He now writes and teaches maths. zipple.co.uk

Ailsa Cox's collection, *The Real Louise and Other Stories*, is published by Headland Press. Stories are included in *Warwick Review, London Magazine and Best British Short Stories 2014*. She lives in Liverpool and teaches at Edge Hill University

Michael Crossan: Novel extract in *Unthology 4* by Unthank Books. Short story winner in the Fish Anthology 2014. Shortlisted for Glimmer Train Open Fiction Prize 2013. Short story shortlisted for Bridport Prize 2011. michaelcwrites.wordpress.com

Sarah Dobbs has a PhD and MA in Creative Writing from Lancaster University. She is a lecturer in Creative Writing at the University of Sunderland and has previously taught at MMU, Edge Hill, Manchester and on the Guardian Masterclass series. She's the founder of Creative Writing the Artist's Way and her debut crime novel, *Killing Daniel*, was published in 2012 by Unthank Books. You can visit her at sarahjanedobbs.wordpress.com @sarahjanedobbs

Tania Hershman is the author of *My Mother Was An Upright Piano: Fictions* (Tangent Books, 2012), and *The White Road and Other Stories* (Salt, 2008) and co-author of *Writing Short Stories: A Writers' & Artists' Companion* (Bloomsbury, 2014). Her debut poetry pamphlet will be published in Feb 2016. www.taniahershman.com

Zoe Lambert's first collection, *The War Tour*, was published by Comma Press in 2011

Aiden O'Reilly's debut short story collection *Greetings, Hero* was published by Honest Publishing UK in 2014. Aiden has worked as a mathematics lecturer, translator, building-site worker, and property magazine editor. His fiction has appeared in *The Stinging Fly, The Dublin Review, The Irish Times, Prairie Schooner, 3am magazine, Unthology* and several anthologies. He won the biannual McLaverty Short Story Award in 2008. He received a bursary from the Arts Council of Ireland in 2012

Dan Powell is a prize-winning author of short fiction and a First Story writer-in-residence. His Scott Prize shortlisted collection, *Looking Out Of Broken Windows*, was also long listed for the Edge Hill Prize. danpowellfiction.com @danpowfiction

Angela Readman's stories have won the National Flash Fiction Day Competition, and The Costa Short Award. Her debut collection *Don't Try This at Home* won a Saboteur Award in 2015, and a Rubery Book Award for short fiction

David Rose made his fictional debut in the Literary Review in 1989; he has published two novels: *Vault* (Salt) and *Meridian* (Unthank Books); and a story collection: *Posthumous Stories* (Salt)

Ashley Stokes is the author of *Touching the Starfish* and *The Syllabus of Errors* (both Unthank Books). He is also editor of *Unthology*

Tim Sykes began writing a couple of years ago. He is working on a series of short stories set in St Petersburg in Russia's topsy-turvy 1990s

Jonathan Taylor's books include the novels *Entertaining Strangers* (Salt, 2012) and *Melissa* (Salt, 2015), the memoir *Take Me Home* (Granta, 2007), and the short-story collection *Kontakte and Other Stories* (Roman, 2013). He is Lecturer in Creative Writing at the University of Leicester. jonathanptaylor.co.uk

u.v.ray writes explosive stories for punks and outsiders in an era of ever increasing sterility. His work has appeared internationally and his books can be found at Murder Slim Press. uvray.moonfruit.com